LIVE

Collected

sona
BOOKS

First Published Danann Publishing Ltd 2019

WARNING: For private domestic use only, any unauthorised Copying, hiring, lending or public performance of this book is illegal.

CAT NO: SON0498

Photography courtesy of

Getty images:

Richard E. Aaron/Redferns	Pete Still/Redferns
Michael Putland	Gary Gershoff
Gijsbert Hanekroot/Redferns	Dave Hogan/Hulton Archive
Anwar Hussein	Kent Gavin/Mirrorpix
Andrew Putler/Redferns	Francesco Prandoni/Redferns
Koh Hasebe/Shinko Music	Dave Hogan
Richard Creamer/Michael Ochs Archives	Jo Hale
ARTCO-Berlin/ullstein bild	Samir Hussein
Rob Verhorst/Redferns	Miquel Llop/NurPhoto
Ross Marino	Rocky Widner/FilmMagic
FG/Bauer-Griffin	Christie Goodwin/Redferns
Michael Montfort/Michael Ochs Archives	

Other images Wiki Commons

Book layout & design Darren Grice at Ctrl-d

Copy Editor Tom O'Neill

Made in EU.

ISBN: 978-1-912918-61-4

Contents

Introduction

'The worst day of my life was once that my mom didn't allow me to go to a Queen concert because I was grounded'

Lars Ulrich of Metallica

For those fortunate enough to have witnessed the classic Queen line-up of front man Freddie Mercury, guitarist Brian May, drummer Roger Taylor and bassist John Deacon playing live, it is an event they never have – and never will – forget. No other rock band – past, present or future – can compare with the power, emotion, theatrics, showmanship and sheer charisma displayed by these four superlative musicians when they took to the stage and to perform some of the best rock and pop songs ever written. In a career spanning 20 years, they played live over 700 times – from early college gigs where they practised at honing their craft to the jaw-dropping, ever-more-spectacular extravaganzas their shows became during their hey-day in the 1970s and 1980s. While nothing can beat the truly awesome event that was seeing classic Queen live, this beautifully illustrated book with over 100 stunning images comes close. . .

1 | The Young Queen on Tour

'We do play to our audience. It's very important. You can't create music in a vacuu

Queen guitarist Brian May

DATES

1971

Jul 2, Surrey College, Surrey, UK

Jul 11, Imperial College, London, UK

Jul 17, The Garden, Penzance, Cornwall, UK

Jul 19, Rugby Club, Hayle, Cornwall, UK

Jul 24, Young Farmers Club, Wadebridge, Cornwall, UK

Jul 29, The Garden, Penzance, Cornwall, UK

Jul 31, City Hall, Truro, Cornwall, UK

Aug 2, Rugby Club, Hayle, Cornwall, UK

Aug 9, Driftwood Spars, St Agnes, Cornwall, UK

Aug 12, Tregye Hotel, Truro, Cornwall, UK

Aug 14, NCO's Mess, RAF Culdrose, Truro, Cornwall, UK

Aug 17, City Hall, Truro, Cornwall

Aug 21, Carnon Downs Festival, Tregye, Cornwall, UK

Oct 6, Imperial College, London, UK

Dec 9, Swimming Baths, Epsom, Surrey, UK

Dec 31, Rugby Club, Twickenham, London, UK

1972

Jan 28, Bedford College, London, UK

Mar 10, King's College Hospital, London, UK

Mar 24, Forest Hill Hospital, London, UK

Nov 6, The Pheasantry Club, Chelsea, London, UK

Dec 20, The Marquee Club, London, UK

1973

Apr 9, Marquee Club, London, UK

Jul 13, Queen Mary College, Basingstoke, Hampshire, UK

Sep 13, Golders Green Hippodrome, London, UK

Oct 13, Bad Godesburg, Frankfurt, West Germany

Oct 14, Le Blow Up Club, Luxembourg

Oct 26, Imperial College, London, UK

Nov 2, Imperial College, London, UK

Typical Set List

While there are no lists from Queen's very early days, what is known is that they played Smile tracks (eg, 'Doing Alright' and 'See What A Fool I've Been'), a couple of their own tracks from the yet-to-be-released debut LP ('Keep Yourself Alive', 'Liar', 'Great King Rat', 'Modern Times Rock n' Roll', 'Son And Daughter'), the never-released track 'Hangman', an early version of 'Stone Cold Crazy', 'Jesus' and 'Night Comes Down' (the latter two were never played live after 1973). Concerts always finished with a medley of Rock n' Roll covers with a typical show lasting approximately 45 minutes.

Queen would never have existed if not for Smile, a three-piece rock band formed in 1968 by three London students – namely, curly-haired, serious-minded guitarist and science student Brian May; bassist Tim Steffel, Brian's old school friend and an art student; and Roger Meddows Taylor, a blonde, angelically-faced trainee dental student, on drums. While attending Art College, Steffel became friendly with exotic, flamboyant, Zanzibar-born fellow-student, Farrokh 'Freddie' Bulsara. Freddie became a 'Smile' fan and when Steffel left the band in 1970, Bulsara suggested that he join as lead singer. He also suggested, some months later, the name of the band be changed to 'Queen'.

'I didn't like the name originally and neither did Brian,' Roger Taylor remarked a few years later. 'But we got used to it. We thought that once we'd got established the music would become the identity more than the name.'

Freddie also made changes to his own name.

'Freddie had written this line in a song called "My Fairy King",' recalls Brian May. 'There's a line in it that says, "Oh Mother Mercury what have you done to me?" It was after that that he said, "I am going to become Mercury as the mother in this song is my mother".'

Numerous, not-very-memorable college gigs followed. There was something missing. The two bass players employed after Steffel's departure simply didn't gel with the rest of the band– one became bored and left of his own accord while the other was sacked for taking centre stage. What was required was a bassist talented enough to play at 'Queen's' musical level while also being a good fit personally. Enter John Deacon – an unassuming electronics student and bass player who had met May and Taylor at a London party in February 1971. He auditioned and landed the gig.

'"Deacy" was just a natural really. We thought he was a spectacular player,' commented guitarist May. 'We were really pleased.'

'Deacy' also fitted in a treat.

'We three were used to each other and so over the top, we thought that because he was so quiet, he would fit in without too much upheaval,' said drummer Roger Taylor.
Even though Deacon's low key on-stage presence was what Queen wanted, he didn't exactly look like the part. Before his debut gig – to which he'd turned up in his usual jeans and T shirt – there was a disagreement over stage-wear. Mercury had picked out a specific shirt he insisted that Deacon don. He was resistant at first but eventually gave in to the flamboyant front man.

Next up was a run of 11 dates in Taylor's native Cornwall. Billed as 'The Legendary Drummer of Cornwall Roger Taylor. . . and Queen', the tour was not without incident. A pub gig ended early due the volume of the PA and the band chased out of the building. Their final gig was an outdoor performance – their first – at Tregye Country Club near Truro, with Queen supporting Hawkwind and Arthur Brown.

'We took a cottage for a fortnight and stayed together,' recalled Deacon. 'It was good because it wasn't long after I joined and we got to know each other really well and it settled us as a group.'

Back in London, Queen's gigs were few and far between from September to December 1971 – their final show of the year being at the London Rugby Club on New Year's Eve. The first show of '72 took place at Bedford College, London on January 28. There were only six paying punters with Deacon remembering it as one of the most embarrassing experiences of his life. The four remaining shows of the year – all London-based – came after Queen had recorded a demo at De Lane Lea Studio. This contained versions of 'Keep Yourself Alive', 'Liar', 'Jesus' and 'The Night Comes Down', and gave the band something concrete, so to speak, with which to contact record companies. The punt paid off. At the Forest Hill gig in March '72, Barry Sheffield of Trident Studios was in the audience. Trident which Barry ran with brother Norman – had started up a record production company and Barry was impressed by the demo. He liked what he saw of Queen on stage which included Freddie's outrageously camped-up rendition of Shirley Bassey's 'Hey Big Spender'. An offer was made and, after months of wrangling over contracts, finally accepted. The deal was that Trident would tout the band around to major recording companies in order to secure a major contract.

Several months were spent recording their first album, 'Queen', however conditions were hardly ideal. The Sheffield brothers stated the band were only allowed to record in 'quiet' periods, ie, when Trident Studios hadn't been booked out by paying artists.

Their next live show came in November 1971 at the Pheasantry in Chelsea but this wasn't a success. The PA system arrived only an hour before Queen were due on stage, causing numerous sound problems.

'It was disastrous,' said Norman Sheffield. 'Four great players – the talent within the four was totally apparent to me. But as a unit it was pretty scruffy.'

A showcase at London's famous Marquee Club the following month hardly fared much better. Jac Holzman, the founder of Elektra Records in the US, flew in especially and was to later write, 'Dreadfully disappointed. I saw nothing on stage to match the power on tape.'

But all was about to change. . . In February 1973, Queen recorded a session for John Peel's 'Sounds of the Seventies' radio show. Two months later, they signed for an undisclosed sum with EMI. The launch gig at the Marquee Club followed on April 9 with Queen performing the following tracks – 'Father to Son', 'Son & Daughter', 'Doing Alright', 'Stone Cold Crazy', 'Keep Yourself Alive', 'Liar', 'Jailhouse Rock' and 'Be Bop A Lulu' as an encore. Holzman was again in the audience and was, this time, impressed. 'We'll do the deal,' he was quoted as saying. 'But tell the guitarist

to make it look harder. Kids like to think it's Beethoven.'

'It really was the embryonic Queen stage act that night,' publicity assistant John Bagnall was to later recall. 'I remember going backstage afterwards and seeing Freddie slumped in the dressing room, physically shattered by the act. What I remember most clearly was that, as he was changing, I saw that his legs were absolutely black with bruises and he explained that that was where he had been slapping his thighs with a tambourine during different numbers. I think that was the first time I ever had a real awareness of how much physical pain and effort could go into such a stage performance.'

By the time, Queen started recording their second album 'Queen II' at Trident that August, they were desperate to play live again. They had performed but a handful of gigs since their Marquee show but were loath to get back on the pub and small club circuit.

'We'd already driven ourselves mad playing pubs and little clubs up and down the country in Smile,' May was quoted as saying. 'We didn't want to go through that again because we thought it would get too depressing.'

On September 13, Queen played Golders Green Hippodrome in London for a BBC 'In Concert' show where they performed most of the material on 'Queen II'. The show opened with a pre-recorded 'Procession' passage recorded for the new album – making this the first time that taped music was heard as part of a live performance. As the house lights dimmed, the band made their way onto the stage before, Mercury, clutching his trademark,

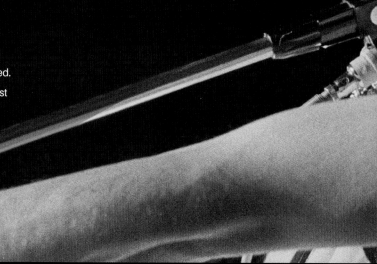

sawn-off 'mic stick', launched into 'Father and Son'. A month later, Queen performed outside the UK for the first time – in Frankfurt, Germany, and then at Le Blow Up Club in Luxembourg.

Two gigs followed at their old stomping ground, London's Imperial College. The first was attended by an EMI executive wanting to check out the company's latest signing. The verdict was that Queen were 'simply amazing – the stage performance was superb as was their music, and the rapport they built up with the audience was fantastic.'

Even more complimentary was the review written by music journalist, Rosemary Horide.

"Sold Out" said the sign on the door. Amazing that an unknown (or almost) group like Queen should sell out a gig at Imperial College. But having seen them now, I understand why. Six months ago, when I last saw the band, they showed promise but weren't very together. This time they were very good. Their leader Freddie Mercury pranced around the small stage, waving his mic both sensually and violently as they performed numbers from their first album, most notable of which were "Keep Yourself Alive" and "Son & Daughter". The atmosphere in the hall was electric, the kids were with Queen all the way, showing a remarkable knowledge of their repertoire and greeting each number uproariously. The group were musically very good, their stage presence was excellent and when you consider that the material was all their own, it was a remarkable performance for a new group. It was obvious how hard the band had worked at entertaining by the tremendous rapport that was established. At the end of the set, after a couple of standard rock n' rollers to provide a fitting climax, the audience wouldn't let Queen go. They were forced on stage to do three encores until they finally had to stop – not from lack of demand but from sheer exhaustion. The funniest moment was undoubtedly the first encore. Freddie's "Big Spender" was done a la Shirley Bassey and thus was outrageously camp. On the whole, it was a good night and a highly credible performance. If Queen are this good on tour with Mott the Hoople which starts next week, Mott had better watch out. Queen could prove to be a bit more than a support band.'

It was prediction that would come true – and then some...

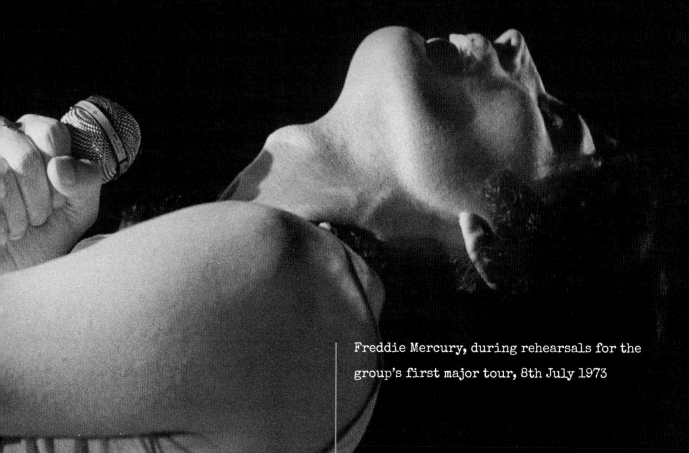

Freddie Mercury, during rehearsals for the group's first major tour, 8th July 1973

2|Queen I Tour

'In the early days, we just wore black onstage. Very bold, my dear. Then we introdu...
white, for variety, and it simply grew and grew'

Freddie Mercury

1973

Nov 12, Town Hall, Leeds, UK

Nov 13, St George's, Blackburn, Lancashire, UK

Nov 15, Gaumont, Worcester, UK

Nov 16, University, Lancaster, UK

Nov 17, Stadium, Liverpool, UK

Nov 18, Victoria Hall, Hanley, Staffordshire, UK

Nov 19, Civic, Wolverhampton, UK

Nov 20, New Theatre, Oxford, UK

Nov 21, Guildhall, Preston, Lancashire, UK

Nov 22, City Hall, Newcastle-Upon-Tyne, UK

Nov 23, Apollo Theatre, Glasgow, UK

Nov 25, Caley Cinema, Edinburgh, UK

Nov 26, Opera House, Manchester, UK

Nov 27, Town Hall, Birmingham, UK

Nov 28, Brangwyn Hall, Swansea, UK

Nov 29, Colston Hall, Bristol, UK

Nov 30, Winter Gardens, Bournemouth, UK

Dec 1, Kursaal, Southend, Essex, UK

Dec 2, Central, Chatham, Kent, UK

Dec 6, Cheltenham College, Cheltenham, UK

Dec 7, Shaftesbury Hall, London, UK

Dec 8, University, Liverpool, UK

Dec 14, Hammersmith Odeon, London, UK

Dec 15, University, Leicester, UK

Dec 21, County Hall, Taunton, Somerset, UK

Dec 22, Town Hall, Peterborough, UK

Dec 28, Top Rank, Liverpool, UK

Feb 2 1974, Sunbury Music Festival, Melbourne, Aus

Typical Set List

'Procession'
'Father to Son'
'Son & Daughter'
'Ogre Battle'
'Hang Man'
'Keep Yourself Alive'
'Liar'
'Jailhouse Rock'
'Shake Rattle & Roll'
'Stupid Cupid'
'Be Bop a Lula'
'Jailhouse Rock' (reprise)
'Big Spender'
'Bama Lama Bama Loo'.

The content of the Rock and Roll medley differed from performance to performance, dependant on the particular 'vibe' of the night.

It was not customary for EMI to pay for one of their up-and-coming acts to appear as 'Special Guests' on another band's tour. Yet they made an exception for Queen, with reports of £10,000 being handed over to Mott The Hoople for the 23-date UK tour. Mott were riding high with hits such as the David Bowie written-and-produced 'All The Young Dudes', 'Honaloochie Boogie' and 'All The Way From Memphis' under their belt.

Queen found their first real experience of life on the road – going from city to city night after night – invigorating and exciting. Although, at times, Freddie, outrageously clad in a plunging, skintight, ankle-length leotard, appeared reserved – possibly in response to the heckling he received from the crowd. At Birmingham Town Hall, for instance, his grand entrance was met with 'F**king get off, ya c**t!' When Freddie spoke between the first and second numbers, he was so polite he could well have been addressing the other Queen – Elizabeth – rather than a rowdy crowd of Mott fans.

'Good evening,' he said. 'We're called Queen. It's so nice to be in Birmingham. There's so many of you, it's lovely. As you've probably gathered, this is the first time we're playing Birmingham and you're very nice (nervous laugh).'

Despite receiving a ketchup-laden hot dog in the face courtesy of the mob in the audience that night, as the tour progressed both Mercury's and the band's confidence grew. Crowds really began to warm to them. After the Glasgow gig, Roger Taylor was heard to say, 'I feel we're really going to make it now. I really feel it's going to happen.' And in Liverpool, they acquired something of a cult following with fans dressing in either all black or all white in homage to their heroes. Meanwhile an American critic noted that Queen were. . . 'A singular and lightly stylised pot-pourri of heavy metal, rococo and English vaudeville themes, soldered together with explosions, dry ice, strobes, spots and a workshop full of technological tricks.'

This tour has gone down in rock annals as the one in which Queen stole the show from Mott. Simple Minds vocalist Jim Kerr, then a teenager attending the Glasgow show, was in no doubt. 'Freddie had black and white clothes on and they delivered an amazing set – they blew Hoople off the stage!' Onstage it was Mercury who was the focal point. The British press largely hated what they saw as his campy, theatrical mannerisms. But he was steadily building a powerful, uncommon bond between the band and its audience, often engaging fans in singalongs. 'What you must understand,' he once told another singer, 'is that my voice comes from the energy of the audience. The better they are, the better I get. The first thing I do in a performance is connect with

the audience. It's about movement, sound, presence and colour. I change when I walk out on stage. I transform into the ultimate showman.'

EMI's then Director of A & R, Bob Mercer remarked that by the end of the 23-date run, Queen were blowing Mott off stage, remarking that the audience had gone nuts. Mercer also recalls a member of the Mott management picking a fight with him because Queen were going down so well.

'He put me up against a wall and said, "They are off the tour. My band will never survive this". And I said, "Sorry sunshine, that's your problem. I paid for them to be here".'

However, there was never any question of the bands themselves not getting on. They travelled on the tour bus together between gigs – with relations remaining cordial even after a Queen fan scrawled 'Mott is dead, long live Queen!' in the dirt on the side of the vehicle on one occasion. And at the Southend gig on December 1, Queen, apart from the painfully shy John Deacon, returned to the stage during Mott's set to contribute backing vocals to 'All The Young Dudes'.

The tour ended on December 14 with two shows at Hammersmith Odeon with Queen pulling out two of their best performances yet to a combined audience of 7000 people – two of whom were Brian May's parents who were astonished at their only son's success. May's dad, Harold, was even asked for his autograph.

The band, Mercury in particular, were now hungry for a taste of playing major venues as headliners.

'The opportunity for playing with Mott was great,' he said at the time. 'But I knew the moment we finished the tour, as far as Britain was concerned, we'd be headlining.'

Thoughts echoed by Queen's then publicist, the late Tony Brainsby.

'Queen may have been a support group but they already had the mentality of stars.'

The band closed the year with four more gigs, culminating with supporting 10CC at Liverpool's Top Rank on December 28. 1973 had been their most successful year to date, the cherry on the cake being Mott asking them to be support on their US tour, due to start in April 1974. The plan was that they would embark on their first headline tour of the UK at the beginning of March to coincide with the release of their second album, 'Queen II'. But first came a disastrous trip to perform at the Sunbury Music Festival in Australia. . .

Queen's appearance at this three-day festival in Melbourne was pretty much doomed from the get-go. Even before leaving the UK, May was in pain due to a travel inoculation with a dirty needle, which caused his arm to swell up like a football and it became gangrenous. Fortunately, the limb was saved but Brian's recovery time meant that the band were unable to rehearse as much as they would have liked. A specially designed lighting rig was flown in from the UK, accompanied by a British crew, which caused problems with Aussie technicians. The rig never worked properly, leading to suspicions of sabotage. The Australian crowd were unhappy that this unknown British band had been given top-billing plus they didn't take kindly to Queen's image with, 'Go back to Pommyland, ya poofters' yelled from the audience at regular intervals. In addition to worry over Brian's arm, Freddie had developed an ear infection which left him unable to hear himself.

Booed off stage, Queen were down but not out.

'When Queen come back to Australia,' vowed Freddie,' we will be the biggest band in the world!'

3|Queen II Tour

I have fun with my clothes onstage: it's not a concert you're seeing, it's a fashion show'

Freddie Mercury

DATES 1974

Mar 1, Winter Gardens, Blackpool
Mar 2, Friars, Aylesbury, Bucks
Mar 3, Guildhall, Plymouth
Mar 4, Festival Hall, Paignton, Devon
Mar 8, Locarno, Sunderland
Mar 9, Corn Exchange, Cambridge
Mar10, Greyhound, Croydon
Mar 12, Roundhouse, Dagenham
Mar 13, Town Hall, Cheltenham
Mar 15, University, Glasgow
Mar 16, University, Stirling
Mar 19, Winter Gardens, Cleethorpes
Mar 20, University, Manchester
Mar 22, Civic Centre, Canvey Island
Mar 23, Links Pavilion, Cromer, Norfolk
Mar 24, Woods Leisure Centre, Colchester
Mar 26, Palace Lido, Douglas, Isle of Man
Mar 28, University, Aberystwyth
Mar 29, the Gardens, Penzance
Mar 39, Century Ballroom, Taunton
Mar 31, Rainbow Theatre, London
Apr 2, Barbarella's, Birmingham

USA

Apr 16, Regis College, Denver, Colorado
Apr 17, Memorial Hall, Kansas City, Missouri
Apr 18, Keil Auditorium, St Louis, Missouri
Apr 19, Fairgrounds Appliance Building, Oklahoma City
Apr 20, Mid-South Coliseum, Memphis, Tennessee
Apr 21, St Bernard Civic Center, New Orleans, Louisiana

Apr 26, Orpheum Theater, Boston, Massachusetts
Apr 27, Palace Theater, Providence, Rhode Island
Apr 28, Exposition Hall, Portland, Maine
May 1, Farm Arena, Harrisburg, Pennsylvania
May 2, Agricultural Hall, Allentown, Pennsylvania
May 4, Palace Theater, Waterbury, Connecticut
May 7,8,9,10,11,12, Uris Theater, New York

Typical Set List

Procession
Father to Son
Ogre Battle
Son and Daughter
Guitar Solo
Son and Daughter (Reprise)
White Queen (As It Began)
Great King Rat
Keep Yourself Alive
Liar
Jailhouse Rock'
Stupid Cupid
Be-Bop-A-Lula
Big Spender
Modern Times Rock n' Roll

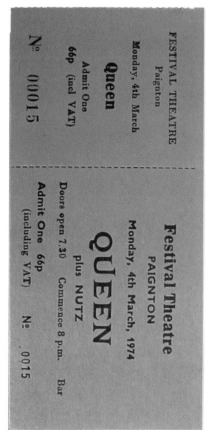

In preparation for their first head-lining tour, Queen – or rather Freddie Mercury – decided to up anti on the on-stage costume stakes. Top fashion designer Zandra Rhodes was chosen to dress them

'It was quite wonderful for me after just dressing ladies to be asked to do something for men,' the designer recalled. 'Freddie would hold things in front of him and just waft around the room.'

She dressed Freddie in a white satin pleated top that would become legendary.

'He tried on several things, modelling them in the studio, but then he tried that on and it was the one. It was actually a piece that had started out as an idea for a wedding dress. So, I said to Freddie, "Move around the room and look in the mirror see how you feel, and if it'll work for you whilst you're on stage". Freddie in my white pleated top went on to become one of the iconic stage images of him.'

For Brian May, meanwhile, Rhodes created a cape in white satin.

Once on the road, the tour wasn't without problems. On the way to the first gig in Blackpool, the vehicle transporting the lighting rig broke down miles from the venue and the show was delayed. Then it was decided to cut some dates as Brian's arm was still proving too painful. The band were also without a support act until Liverpool combo Nutz joined them several gigs in. After the Croydon gig, Freddie was convinced he was losing his mind. 'I'm breaking down,' he told one reporter. 'I'm so fatigued.' Perhaps it was this exhaustion that explained the occasional hissy fit. After one night, for instance, he threw a glass at one of the crew. Taylor and May also argued, with the drummer squirting hairspray in the guitarist's face. After the Cheltenham gig, the lighting team unexpectedly quit and had to be replaced at very short notice. Then two nights later, in Stirling, Scotland, the police were called after the audience started to riot when Queen wouldn't play a fourth encore. Two people were stabbed and two members of the crew also hurt. The band locked themselves in the back-stage

kitchen until it was safe to leave. The next gig in Birmingham was cancelled and tacked on to the end of the tour. A later gig in the Isle of Man, in which a hotel room was trashed, added to the band's negative headlines in the press.

On a happier note 'Queen II', released on March 8, reached number five in the UK album charts and this was reflected in ticket sales. It was also during this tour – at the Plymouth gig to be exact – that the audience started to sing 'God Save The Queen' while waiting for an encore. This led to Queen recording an arrangement of the British national anthem which would then be used to conclude every show.

The penultimate live performance on the tour was at the sold-out Rainbow Theatre in London – the venue where Jimi Hendrix had famously set fire to his guitar several years before – but tempers were beginning to spark again.

'Roger was planning to wear some top that Freddie wanted to wear that night,' recalls a member of support band, Nutz. 'Freddie was furious. During the sound check, he threw down the mic and stormed off. I think he went and sat in the van. Brian turned up volume and said over the mic – "Freddie dear come back you, old queen. Come back and sound check." Freddie was then furious with Brian, as well.'

During the show, there was a complete power breakdown but the 3,500 capacity crowd waited patiently until normal service was resumed. Freddie, his earlier mood forgotten, was in fine form – prowling up and down the stage like a big cat, tossing back his mane of black hair as he sidled up first to May and then Deacon. At one point between songs, he disappeared from stage only to reappear having swapped his white tunic for a black, slashed top. At the end of the show, he tossed a pair of flower handcuffs into the audience.

'A riveting performer,' was music newspaper Melody Maker's verdict. 'The stuff idols are made of.'

Once again, music scribe Rosemary Horide was full of compliments.

'What a night!' she wrote. 'It was a finale of the big Queen tour throughout the whole country... it was a conclusive evening for their reputation. Their lift was meteoric, so many people had challenged whether Queen had the authority to play in such a prestigious place as the Rainbow. Freddie appeared in his new especially eccentric white "eagle" costume while bouncing and mining with even bigger ecstasy than ever and sang even better than any time before.. One couldn't believe this was the first Queen appearance in such an important place. After a while they got used to taking advantage of the big stage. After two encores they left the stage to big applause from the audience.'

Backstage, the band received the best compliment. Simon Townsend, the 13-year-old brother of The Who's Pete, announced that Queen were 'much better than my brother's band'. Freddie was reportedly ecstatic to hear this.

The tour concluded with the rearranged Birmingham gig, at Barberella's where Freddie strutted flamboyantly along the catwalk. In typical last-night-of-the-tour high spirits, the Nutz singer and crew stripped and streaked across the stage behind Freddie as Queen performed, having been egged on by Roger Taylor and the promise of a bottle of champagne.

'I knew something was going on,' Freddie was later to say. 'For the first time, the audience were not looking at me.'

Queen played their first gig in the USA – once again supporting Mott the Hoople – on April 16. The Queen II album had been released a week earlier and reached a respectable 49 in the charts. However, the early reviews of their live shows stateside weren't great.

'Queen's on-stage presence an almost laughable bizarre mish-mash of every other successful band of their era,' read one. While another sneered, 'They are doing nothing special, there are

Queen on stage, 1974. L-R Brian May, John Deacon, Roger Taylor and Freddie Mercury

moments when they sound influenced by The Who and moments when they are nearer Zeppelin.'

But by April 27, Queen had hit their stride and even had a fan in Mott's drummer, Dale Griffin.

'Queen are not a sabotage band,' he said at the time. 'We have had to work with some in the past, roadies who fall over leads and pulling them out accidentally on purpose. The concert itself is excellent – one of best I've seen in ages. Freddie Mercury parodies everyone but has style and gets away with it.'

The name of the band was enough on its own to attract attention from a more outrageous kind of audience.

'We thought we were unusual but a lot of people that came to see us were surprising even to us,' revealed Brian May. 'Transvestite artists, the New York Dolls, Andy Warhol – people that were creative in a way that appeared to trash everything that had gone before.'

The harmonious atmosphere of the tour was jeopardised when Aerosmith were added to the bill in Harrisburg, Pennsylvania. There were arguments over which support band should go on first. Guitarists Brian May and Joe Perry did not care, preferring to share a bottle of Jack Daniels rather than join in the war of words. May later said that he played the entire gig on automatic pilot. Under the influence of alcohol, he was far more flamboyant than usual – something his bandmates complimented him on and from then on, he incorporated this showier element into future performances.

As the tour continued, an element of 'one upmanship' was creeping in. Freddie was as mesmerising as always but Brian was also developing a special on-stage charisma and certain members of Mott's crew weren't happy.

'Brian had his Zandra Rhodes costume on in New York,' recalled a record company executive. 'The idea was that when he hit the big Pete Townsend windmill chord, the lighting engineer knew to put a spot on him which would catch the pleats of the tunic. It was a beautiful effect. One of Mott's crew knew this and started trashing the board, hitting all the faders to throw him off his mark.'

Meanwhile Freddie was delighted at the adoration he was receiving from the audience.

'We played a theatre in New York with Mott and this particular chick (well, they notice everything down to the pimple on your arse, dear) wrote that she noticed that when I did a costume change I changed even my shoes and socks. She also added she was so close she could tell what religion I was, and that I wasn't wearing any knickers,' he told one writer.

It was after the final New York show that Brian May collapsed. He seemed to recover but waking up in Boston the next morning, could barely move. It was initially thought he was suffering from food poisoning but hepatitis was diagnosed. The combination of his still-infected arm, late nights, stress from touring and a poor diet had proved truly toxic. There was no way he could continue the tour. Queen were forced to fly back to the UK and May ordered to spend six weeks on bed rest.

The US live shows were rescheduled for July but were again cancelled when May was diagnosed with a duodenal ulcer which required surgery.

'Brian has got to look after himself in future,' Freddie was quoted as saying to the New Musical Express. 'We all want to make sure something like that never happens again. So, he'll have to eat the right things and steer clear of hamburgers.'

Queen on stage in London, 1974. L–R John Deacon, Freddie Mercury, Roger Taylor and Brian May

4 | Sheer Heart Attack Tour

'Each gig should be unique. You're always treading that line betwee[n] keeping yourself fresh and giving people something they want to hear

Brian May

1974

UK

Oct 30, Palace Theatre, Manchester
Oct 31, Victoria Hall, Hanley, Staffordshire
Nov 1, Liverpool Empire, Liverpool
Nov 2, Leeds University, Leeds
Nov 3, Belgrade Theatre, Coventry
Nov 5, City Hall, Sheffield
Nov 6, St George's Hall, Bradford
Nov 7, City Hall, Newcastle-upon-Tyne
Nov 8, Apollo Theatre, Glasgow
Nov 9, University, Lancaster
Nov 10, Guildhall, Preston
Nov 12, Colston Hall, Bristol
Nov 13, Winter Gardens, Bournemouth
Nov 14, Gaumont, Southampton
Nov 15, Brangwyn Hall, Swansea
Nov 16, Town Hall, Birmingham
Nov 18, New Theatre, Oxford
Nov 19/20, Rainbow Theatre, London

Europe

Nov 23, Gothenburg, Sweden
Nov 25, Helsingen Kuittuuritalo, Helsinki
Dec 1, 140 Theatre, Brussels
Dec 2, Munich, Germany
Dec 4, Frankfurt, Germany
Dec 5, Hamburg, Germany
Dec 6, Cologne, Germany
Dec 7, Siegan, Germany
Dec 8, Congress Gebouw, The Hague, Holland
Dec 10, Barcelona, Spain

1975

North America

Feb 5, Agora, Columbus, Ohio
Feb 6, Palace Theater, Dayton, Ohio
Feb 8, Music Hall, Cleveland, Ohio
Feb 9, Morris Civic Auditorium, South Bend, Indiana
Feb 10, Ford Auditorium, Detroit, Michigan
Feb 11, Student Union Auditorium, Toledo, Ohio
Feb 14, Palace Theater, Waterbury, Connecticut
Feb 15, Orpheum Theater, Boston
Feb 16, Avery Fisher Hall, New York
Feb 17, War Memorial, Trenton, New Jersey
Feb 19, Lewiston, New York
Feb 21, Capitol Theater, Passaic, New Jersey
Feb 22, Farm Arena, Harrisburg, Pennsylvania
Feb 23, Erlinger Theater, Philadelphia, Pennsylvania
Feb 24, Kennedy Center, Washington, Pennsylvania

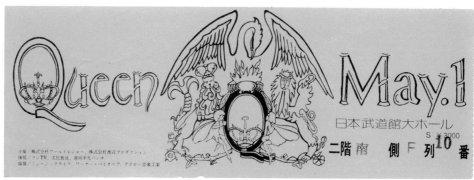

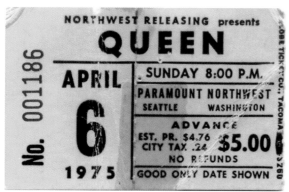

Typical Set List

Procession
Now I'm Here
Ogre Battle
Father to Son
White Queen
Flick of the Wrist
In the Lap of the Gods
Killer Queen
March of the Black Queen
Bring Back That Leroy Brown
Son and Daughter
Keep Yourself Alive
Seven Seas of Rhye
Stone Cold Crazy
Liar
Big Spender
Modern Times Rock n' Roll
Jailhouse Rock
God Save The Queen

Mar 5, Mary E Sawyer Auditorium, La Crosse, Wisconsin
Mar 6, Madison, Wisconsin
Mar 7, Uptown Theater, Milwaukee, Wisconsin
Mar 8, Aragon Ballroom, Chicago, Illinois
Mar 9, Keil Auditorium, St Louis, Missouri
Mar 10, Coliseum, Fort Wayne, Indiana
Mar 12, Municipal Auditorium, Atlanta, Georgia
Mar 13, Civic Auditorium, Charleston, South Carolina
Mar 15, Marina, Miami, Florida
Mar 18, St Bernard Civic Auditorium, New Orleans, Lousiana
Mar 20, Municipal Hall, San Antonio, Texas
Mar 23, McFarlin Auditorium, Dallas, Texas
Mar 25, Municipal Theater, Tulsa, Oklahoma
Mar 29, Santa Monica Civic Auditorium, Los Angeles
Mar 30, Winterland, San Francisco, California
Apr 2, Kindmens Fieldhouse, Edmonton, Alberta
Apr 3, Calgary, Alberta
Apr 6, Seattle, Washington

Japan

Apr 19, Budokan Hall, Tokyo
Apr 22, Aichi Taiikukan, Nagoya
Apr 23, Nokusai Talkan, Kobe
Apr 25, Kyden Taiikukan, Fukuoka
Apr 28, Taiikukan, Okayama
Apr 29, Yamaha Tsumagoi Hall, Shizuoka
Apr 30, Bunkan Taiikukan, Yokahama
May 1, Budokan Hall, Tokyo

Queen's third album 'Sheer Heart Attack', featuring the smash-hit singles 'Now I'm Here' and 'Killer Queen' was released on November 8 in the UK and on November 12 in the US, reaching chart positions 2 and 12, respectively. On October 30, they'd embarked on their first world tour. It was at the first gig on this tour – in Manchester – that they first played their special recording of 'God Save The Queen'. Production values had stepped up a notch on the SHA tour with an impressive light show and fireworks closing proceedings every night. Audiences loved the rock and roll dazzle of it all. Freddie's stage look was, once again, an innovation. His all-white outfit was accessorised by chainmail effect gauntlet on his left-hand. Midway through the set, he'd change costume and emerge in head-to-toe black, complete with leather gloves accessorised with talons.

'Do you like my claws?' he'd purr to the crowd.

The rest of the band also rocked a monochrome look. John Deacon wore the typical 1970s velvet jacket- and-flared trouser combo, Brian May sported a white-caped outfit while Roger, as drummer, opted for the more practical baggy shirt or T-shirt with jeans.

The gig at Liverpool Empire has gone down in Queen history as one of their best ever shows. A local newspaper the next day reported, 'The audience were standing up to desperately gaze at the darkened, empty stage, and there they were... shadowy figures bounding towards the waiting instruments. The lights blazed and there was evil Freddie, clad all in white, the archetypal demon jock singer, pointing and snarling, "Queen is back! What do you think of that?".'

However, this British leg of the tour wasn't problem-free. At the Leeds gig, Roger Taylor's on-stage monitor failed and, once back in the dressing room, the drummer kicked the wall so forcefully, his foot was badly bruised and he needed hospital attention. Scuffles also broke out in the crowd at Leeds but Freddie Mercury managed to calm things down from the stage so that another Stirling situation was avoided. The Glasgow show also threatened to erupt into something dangerous as Freddie was dragged into the audience by the crowd. He was promptly dragged back out again by security.

Queen were originally only scheduled to play one night at London's Rainbow Theatre but such was the demand for tickets, a second night was added. Both shows sold-out. The second show was sound recorded and filmed – the first time the band were filmed live in concert. Freddie's first words to the crowd were, 'The nasty Queenies are back – what do you think of that? It's been so long we've missed you all – we really have. Have you missed us?'

At the end of the British leg of the tour, Queen were presented with a plaque for selling out every gig and voted 'Best Live Act' 1974 by readers of the Sun newspaper.

The European dates in Scandinavia, Belgium, Germany and Spain were also selling out as sales of 'Sheer Heart Attack' album continued to soar. However, the European shows themselves were not entirely successful.

'For the first time in many months I felt like I'd done a hard day's work when I came off stage – we were getting nothing back,' recalled Brian May.

At the gig in Munich, the venue was rammed with GIS from a nearby US airbase who much preferred support band, Lynyrd Skynyd of 'Sweet Home Alabama' fame. LS didn't 'get' Queen, either.

'They couldn't believe it when they saw us four caked in make-up and dressed like women,' said Roger Taylor.

When Queen were on stage, they were heckled by the support band's management, who held aloft posters on which were written 'Shit!' and 'Queen Suck!' After the third German date, the American band were kicked off the tour.

Freddie Mercury on stage at Congres Gebouw
on 8th December 1974 in The Hague, Netherlands

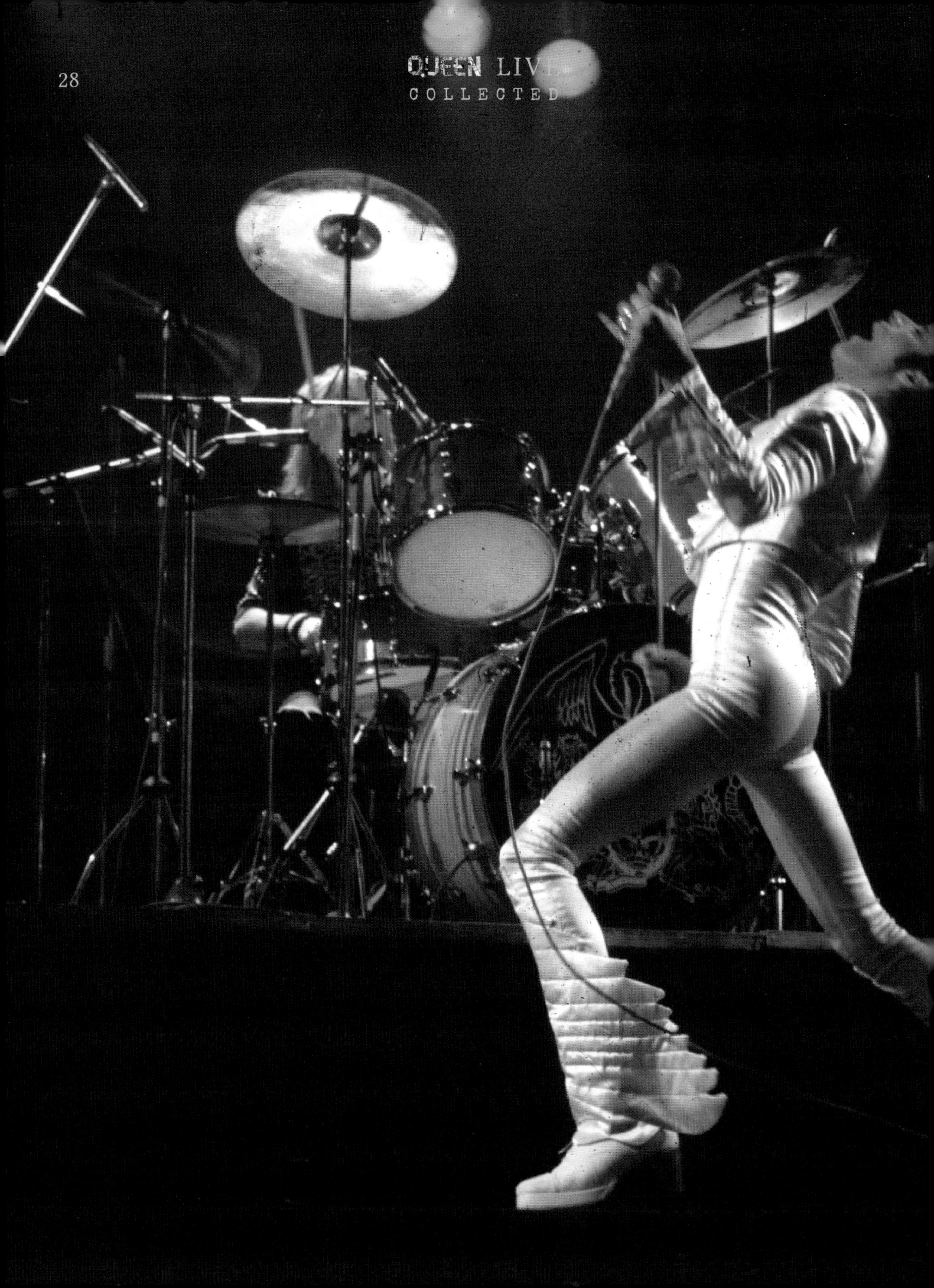

1975 dawned and it was time to make up for those cancelled US tour dates.

'We were confident we would go down alright in the east & Midwest but not too expect too much in South and far west,' remembers Roger Taylor.

After a week's rehearsal in New York, road-testing a new PA and lighting rig, Queen kicked off their 38 show, 30 venue US tour – their first as headliners. But three weeks in, there were problems with Freddie's throat. After losing his voice entirely after the Philadelphia show, he was diagnosed with possible nodules on his throat and told to rest. There was fat chance of that, although at the next show in Washington DC, he refrained from scaling the highest notes. He was distraught, vowing to 'sing until my throat is like a vulture's crotch'.

'They went on stage and did the most amazing gig that I have ever seen them do in my life,' remembers one of their entourage. 'It was amazing because they seemed to have so much energy and to my astonishment, Freddie was hitting the high notes again'.

But he was in agony and the rest of the band were informed after the gig that there would be no more shows for three months. Six concerts – Pittsburgh, Kurzon, Buffalo, Toronto, London Ontario & Davenport – were immediately cancelled. The tour resumed on March 5 as Freddie's condition turned out to be down to severe swelling rather than throat nodules diagnosed. In an attempt to save his voice, he refrained from his usual on-stage banter. By the Chicago date, he seemed back on top of his game with a Melody Maker reporter remarking on his mic technique.

'He plays it like a guitar, aims it at the audience rifle fashion, wields it like a samurai sword and pretends to break it across his knee like an apache declaring war.'

However, the tour limped rather than raced towards the finish with more shows being cancelled due to Freddie's on-going vocal problems. Yet again Queen's stateside outing had been stymied by a member's failing health. Their Japanese experience went some way to make up for it, though.

On April 18, they were overwhelmed to arrive at Tokyo airport where 3000 screaming fans were waiting to greet them. Pandemonium broke out. It was like Beatlemania.

'We couldn't take it in,' remembers Brian May. 'It was like another world. Something just clicked in Japan. Suddenly we were the Beatles.'

The eight dates were bookended by shows at the world-famous Budukan Hall, a venue with a 14,200 capacity. At the first show, Sumo wrestlers stood guard in order to stop fans from invading the stage and at one point Freddie was forced to stop proceedings as the crowd were becoming dangerously over-excited.

'The noise was enormous,' John Deacon remembered. 'There was so much screaming and throwing presents.'

For the Japanese shows, 'Hangman', 'Great King Rat', 'Doin' All Right' and 'See What A Fool I've Been' were worked into the set. At their penultimate gig in Japan, Queen came on stage wearing kimonos – the national dress of Japan – which drove fans mad with delight. As they left the country, their single 'Killer Queen' and the Sheer Heart Attack album were topping the charts. Japan had changed everything. . .

Freddie Mercury of Queen performing on stage 1975 in London

5 | A Night at the Opera Tour

'Queen Invite You To A Night At The Opera'

Wording on the tour programme cover

1975

UK

Nov 14/15, Empire Theatre, Liverpool
Nov 16, Belgrade Theatre, Coventry
Nov 17/18, Colston Hall, Bristol
Nov 19, Capitol Theatre, Cardiff
Nov 21, Odeon, Taunton
Nov 23, Winter Gardens, Bournemouth
Nov 24, Gaumont, Southampton
Nov 26, Free Trade Hall, Manchester
Nov 29/30 & December 1/2, Hammersmith Odeon, London
Dec 7, Civic Hall, Wolverhampton
Dec 8, Guildhall, Preston
Dec 9/10, Odeon, Birmingham
Dec 11, City Hall, Newcastle-upon-Tyne
Dec 13, Caird Hall, Dundee
Dec 14, Capitol, Aberdeen
Dec 15/16, Apollo, Glasgow
Dec 24, Hammersmith Odeon, London

1976

North America

Jan 27, Palace Theater, Waterbury, Connecticut
Jan 29/30, Music Hall, Boston, Massachusetts
Jan 31 & February 1, Tower Theater, Philadelphia,
Feb 5/6/7/8, Beacon Theater, New York

Feb 11/12, Masonic Temple, Detroit, Michigan
Feb13, Riverfront Coliseum, Cincinnati, Ohio
Feb14, Public Hall, Cleveland, Ohio
Feb 15, Sports Arena, Toledo, Ohio
Feb 18, Civic Center, Saginaw,Michigan
Feb 19, Veterans' Memorial Auditorium, Columbus, Ohio
Feb 20, Syrian Mosque. Pittsburgh, Pennsylvania
Feb 22/23 Auditorium Theater, Chicago, Illinois
Feb 26, Keil Auditorium, St Louis, Missouri
Feb 27, Convention Center, Indianapolis, Indiana
Feb 28, Dane County Coliseum, Wisconsin
Feb 29, Fort Wayne Coliseum, Indiana State
Mar 1, Milwaukee Auditorium, Wisconsin
Mar 3, St Pauls Auditorium, Minneapolis, Minnesota
Mar 7, Berkeley Community Hall, Berkeley
Mar 9/10/11/12, Santa Monica Civic Auditorium, LA
Mar 13, Sports Arena, San Diego

Japan

Mar 22, Budokan Hall, Tokyo
Mar 23, Aichi Ken Gynmasium, Nagoya
Mar 24, Kosei Kaikan, Himeji City
Mar 26, Kyden Gymnasium, Fukuoka
Mar 29, Kosei Nenkin Kaikan, Osaka
Mar 31 & April 1, Budokan Hall, Tokyo
Apr 2, Miyagi Sports Centre, Sendai
Apr 4, Nichidai Kodo, Tokyo

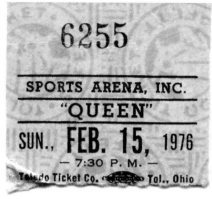

Australia

Apr 11, Entertainment Centre, Perth
Apr 14/15, Apollo Stadium, Adelaide
Apr 17/18, Horden Pavillion, Sydney
Apr 19/20, Festival Hall, Melbourne
Apr 22, Festival Hall, Brisbane

Plus...

Sep 1/2, Playhouse Theatre, Edinburgh, Scotland
Sep 10, Cardiff Castle, Cardiff, Wales
Sep 18, Hyde Park, London

Having recorded their fourth album – which included the epic game-changer single that would be 'Bohemian Rhapsody' – over summer 1975, Queen embarked on their third head-lining tour. They opened at Liverpool Empire on November 14 to a sell-out audience and an ecstatic reception. Eleven days later, news broke that 'Bohemian Rhapsody' was at number one. It was to stay in the UK charts for 17 weeks, nine of them at the top.

Actual opera had nothing on this production. The stage set included more lights, magnesium flares, special effects and dry ice than ever before. A massive gong was added to Roger Taylor's drum kit – an affectionate parody of the Rank Organisation's signature gong at the start of their movies – which he struck just once at the end of 'Bohemian Rhapsody'. On a smaller scale but no less dramatic, Taylor's snare drum was filled with lager to create a golden fountain of liquid during his solo.

The show began with taped introduction by Freddie's best friend, DJ Kenny Everett, in which he announced, 'Ladies and gentleman, a Night at the Opera...' A recording of the operatic section of 'Bohemian Rhapsody was played before band came on stage. It was then reprised several numbers in and finally played in completion later in the set. During the operatic interlude, the band rushed off stage to change – Freddie, black polish on his finger nails, swapping his winged Hermes suit for a slash-necked black top, decorated with diamonds on chains, and tiny, skin-tight satin shorts.

'Rude? Meant to be, dear,' he quipped to one journalist.

On the third night of the tour, in Coventry, he went on stage in a kimono in tribute to his Japanese fans. The English fans were delighted. Meanwhile Brian's costumes, while not so flamboyant, were just as impressive - usually skin-tight silk or satin trousers with flowing embroidered tops, John and Roger wore similar garb.

The tour was a triumph - ecstatic responses from audiences and rave reviews from the critics. One review read, 'Freddie reacts to his audience like an over emotional actress - Gloria Swanson, Bette Davies. At the second night in Bristol, he paused at the top of the drum stand, looked back at crowd and with complete, heartfelt emotion blew a kiss. In true operatic diva style, he also took to throwing carnations and roses into the audience at the end of a show.'

But even better was yet to come. . . Having played five sell-out nights at London's Hammersmith Odeon from 29th November to 3rd December, Queen continued their triumphant procession around the country, returning to Hammersmith Odeon for a very special gig on Christmas Eve. For the first time ever, BBC's flagship TV music show 'The Old Grey Whistle Test' filmed a rock concert and broadcast it live, while it aired simultaneously in stereo on Radio One. It was a triumph. Not only were the 3500 fans lucky enough to get tickets able to see a remarkable concert, but many hundreds of thousands more were able to celebrate Christmas by experiencing a landmark in rock music on TV.

Freddie looked truly spectacular in skin-tight white satin suit with a matching short jacket and white boots. Brian, too, was in head-to-toe white - namely a Zandra Rhodes-designed cloak. John Deacon wore white trousers and waistcoat and black shirt. Queen rose to the challenge with a high-octane performance that almost blew the roof off the famous venue. Freddie pranced and prowled around the stage, manipulating the audience with ease as his extraordinary voice interpreted the songs. Brian strutted and posed as his pure and incredible guitar-playing filled the hall. John laid down a strong and steady foundation for the songs, while Roger, the other half of the band's rhythmic 'engine room', played an extraordinary set on drums and other percussion, providing another focal point at the back of the stage.

A DVD has been taken from this Christmas Eve concert. 'It's quite something to watch,' said Brian May. 'We were just a four-piece, but we made a lot of noise. I'm quite shocked at how good it was. We were incredibly tight and, at the same time - because we knew each other so well - very loose in terms of improvisation.'

There were many truly memorable moments from the concert, such as when Freddie seemed to be in two places at once during the song 'Now I'm Here'. The band's then personal manager, who was a similar build to Mercury, dressed up as the front man and appeared on stage simultaneously. The show ended with hundreds of festively-themed balloons dropping from the ceiling. A number of blow-up dolls also made the journey! As the final notes of the encores finally died away, Queen realised that they really had arrived at the top of the UK rock hierarchy. As 1975 drew to a close, 'A Night at the Opera' reached number one. Next stop the rest of the world. As they left for their US tour in January 1976, Queen could only reflect back on what had been an amazing year.

As Queen arrived in the US, 'Bohemian Rhapsody' was at number 59 in the charts. The band were a substantially bigger act than they had been a year earlier and the tour saw them playing larger venues such as New York's Beacon Theater where they performed for four nights. Between songs, Freddie threw thornless roses into the crowd and raised his flute of champagne to them. For the first time in North America, the band experienced no health issues and their final four nights in LA were a triumph. The American press approved of their 'purist hard rock' with some publications comparing them to the Beatles. It was predicted that the band would be filling 10,000 seaters when they next toured. By the end of the 33 date North American leg of the tour,

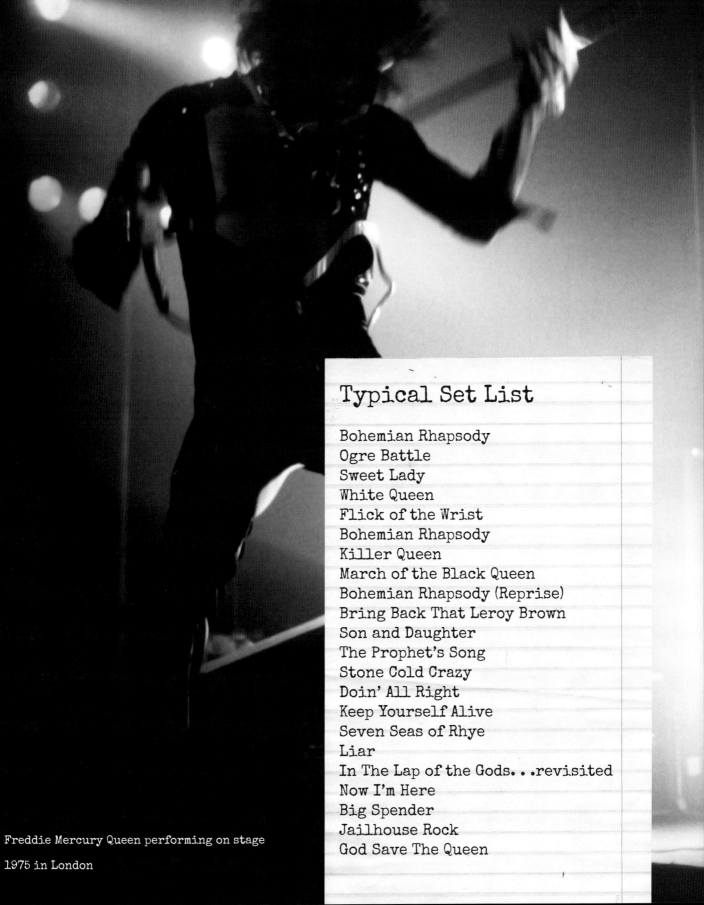

Typical Set List

Bohemian Rhapsody
Ogre Battle
Sweet Lady
White Queen
Flick of the Wrist
Bohemian Rhapsody
Killer Queen
March of the Black Queen
Bohemian Rhapsody (Reprise)
Bring Back That Leroy Brown
Son and Daughter
The Prophet's Song
Stone Cold Crazy
Doin' All Right
Keep Yourself Alive
Seven Seas of Rhye
Liar
In The Lap of the Gods...revisited
Now I'm Here
Big Spender
Jailhouse Rock
God Save The Queen

Freddie Mercury Queen performing on stage
1975 in London

'Bohemian Rhapsody' had reached number nine in the charts.

A tour of Japan followed with the reception being even more ecstatic than the year before. Both Brian May and Freddie Mercury had learned a little of the language, sending the fans even wilder with appreciation.

'Thank-you. . .Origato. . .Sinara. . .Goodbye,' is how Freddie bade farewell before the recording of 'God Save The Queen' was broadcast.

Once again, they received rave reviews.

'When Queen landed recently for an extensive tour of the land of the Rising Sun, the rhapsodic quartet found their plane surrounded by 5,000 frantic fans,' wrote New York magazine, 'Back Pages'.

Queen undoubtedly ruled in Japan. The nation's top radio stations voted them the world's number one rock band and their 12-day tour included three, sell-out nights at the Budokan.

From Japan, the band travelled to Australia – their first trip back since the ill-fated Sunbury Festival two years before. While falling some way short of being the biggest band in the world, as Freddie had vowed they would be when they returned Down Under, the band were triumphant. Both 'Bohemian Rhapsody and 'A Night at the Opera' were chart-toppers reached and all the dates were a sell-out.

Returning to the UK in the spring, by July Queen had begun work on their next album, 'A Day at the Races'. Realising a planned summer '76 release would not be possible, they agreed to play two open air shows and two nights in a theatre throughout late summer/early autumn 1976. As part of the Scottish Festival of Popular Music, they played two dates at the newly refurbished Playhouse Theatre in Edinburgh while at Cardiff Castle, Queen were joined onstage by Manfred Man's Earth band, Frankie Miller and Andy Fairweather-Low. Two new songs were given their first public airing – 'You Take My Breath Away' and 'Tie Your Mother Down.'

'Queen don't worry about about competition. Queen don't worry about anything,' read a Record Mirror review.

The free Hyde Park Show followed a week later on the sixth anniversary of Jimi Hendrix's death. Over 150,000 people filled the park for the concert which had come close to being cancelled due to drought.

'Welcome to our picnic by the Serpertine,' were Freddie's first words to the massive crowd as he strutted across the stage in a black open-to-the-navel leotard and ballet shoes. The gig didn't exactly end as expected with Queen's set being cut short by 30 minutes as they'd overrun. Freddie was determined to go back on stage – until police warned he would be immediately arrested if he attempted it.

'The thought of being in jail in tights didn't appeal to Freddie at all,' recalled then tour manager, Gerry Stickells.

Queen live at Nihon Budokan, Tokyo, March 22, 1976

6 | A Day at The Races Tour

*'You motherf**kers'*

Freddie Mercury's response to being pelted with eggs while on stage in Chicago

1977

North America

Jan 13, Auditorium, Milwaukee, Wisconsin

Jan 14, Dane County Coliseum, Madison, Wisconsin

Jan 15, Columbus Gardens, Columbus, Indiana

Jan 16, Convention Centre, Indianapolis, Indiana

Jan 18, Cobo Hall, Detroit, Michigan

Jan 20, Civic Center, Saginaw, Michigan,

Jan 21, Elliot Hall of Music, Louisville, Kentucky

Jan 22, Wings Stadium, Kalamazoo, Michigan

Jan 23, Richfield Coliseum, Cleveland, Ohio

Jan 25, Central Canadian Exhibition, Ottawa, Ontario

Jan 26, The Forum, Montreal, Quebec

Jan 28, Chicago Stadium, Chicago, Illinois

Jan 30, St John's Arena, Toledo, Ohio

Feb 1, Maple Leaf Gardens, Toronto, Ontario

Feb 3, Civic Center, Springfield, Massachusetts

Feb 4, College Park, University of Maryland

Feb 5, Madison Square Garden, New York

Feb 6, Nassau Coliseum, Nassau, The Bahamas

Feb 8, War Memorial Auditorium, Syracuse, New York

Feb 9, Boston Garden, Boston, Massachusetts

Feb 10, Civic Center, Providence, Rhode Island

Feb 11, Civic Center, Philadelphia, Pennsylvania

Feb 19, Spectorium, Miami, Florida

Feb 20, Civic Center, Lakeland, Florida

Feb 21, Fox Theater, Atlanta, Georgia

Feb 22, Auditorium, Birmingham, Alabama

Feb 24, Kiel Auditorium, St Louis, Missouri

Feb 25, Lloyd Noble Center, Norman, Oklahoma

Feb 26, Moody Coliseum, Dallas, Texas

Feb 27, Sam Houston, Houston, Texas

Mar 1, Phoenix Coliseum, Phoenix, Arizona

Mar 3/4, Inglewood Forum, Los Angeles

Mar 16/17/18, Jubilee Auditorium, Calgary, Alberta

Europe and UK

May 13, Congresscentrum, Hamburg

May 14, Jahrhunderthalle, Frankfurt

May 16, Philipshalle, Dusseldorf

May 17, Ahoy Hall, Rotterdam

May 19, Sporthalle, Basle

May 23/4, Hippodrome, Bristol

May 26/27, Gaumont, Southampton

May 29, Bingley Hall, Stafford

May 30/31, Apollo, Glasgow

Jun 2/3, Empire Theatre, Liverpool

Jun 6/7, Earls Court, London

Tisdag
10 maj 1977
kl. 19.30

SEKTION
HÖGER
B

QUEEN

KR 35:—

Betald biljett återtages ej.
Förköp 1:50

SCANDINAVIUM

RAD | PLATS
18 16

Lippmann + Rau
Concertbüro GmbH + Co., KG

QUEEN
in Concert
+ Vorprogramm

14. Mai
1977
20 Uhr
20,—

Samstag   14. Mai 1977   20 Uhr

Festhalle - Messe
Frankfurt   DM 20,—
+ Vorverkaufsgebühr, incl. 5,5 % MWSt.

Erdgeschoß
Ground Floor   № 01819

druckerei MERKUR, Frankfurt-Niedereschbach

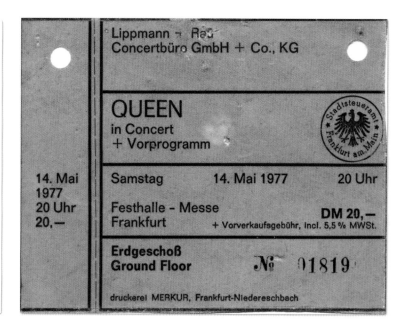

EARLS COURT, LONDON
(Opposite Warwick Road Exit, Earls Court Tube Station)

Harvey Goldsmith and John Reid
cordially invite you to a night with

Queen

BLOCK
19

MONDAY, 6th JUNE, 1977
at 8.00 p.m.

Ground Floor Stalls £4.00

For Conditions of Sale see over

DD22

To be retained

SEC.   ROW   SEAT
51   A   8
EAST

Retain Stub - Good Only
No Exchange — No Refund

TUE.
8:00 P.M.   **FEB. 1**
Davis Printing Limited   1977

"QUEEN"
PRICE-7.00+RST .70-$7.70

ADMIT ONE. Entrance by Main
Door or by Church Street Door.

Maple Leaf Gardens
LIMITED
CONDITION OF SALE

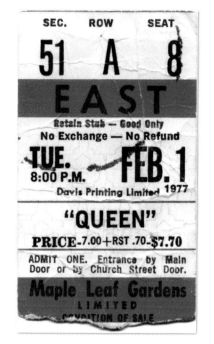

WEST BALCONY
SEC   ROW   SEAT
W19   3   14
FEB. 26, 1977
ADMIT ONE ON ABOVE DATE ONLY

KILT & CONCERTS WEST
PRESENT

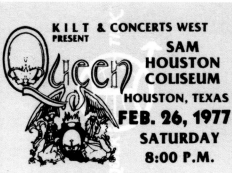
Queen

**SAM
HOUSTON
COLISEUM**
HOUSTON, TEXAS
FEB. 26, 1977
SATURDAY
8:00 P.M.

NO REFUND   PRICE   NO EXCHANGE
$7.00

SEC   ROW   SEAT
W19   3   14
WEST BALCONY

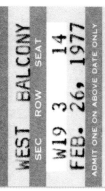

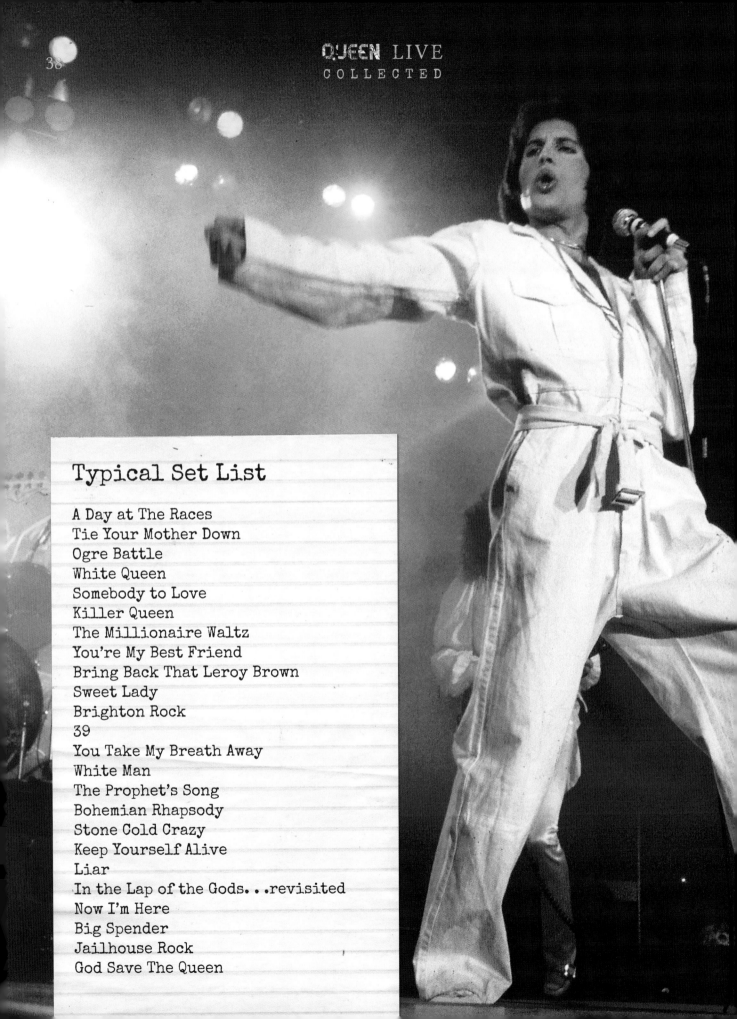

Typical Set List

A Day at The Races
Tie Your Mother Down
Ogre Battle
White Queen
Somebody to Love
Killer Queen
The Millionaire Waltz
You're My Best Friend
Bring Back That Leroy Brown
Sweet Lady
Brighton Rock
39
You Take My Breath Away
White Man
The Prophet's Song
Bohemian Rhapsody
Stone Cold Crazy
Keep Yourself Alive
Liar
In the Lap of the Gods. . .revisited
Now I'm Here
Big Spender
Jailhouse Rock
God Save The Queen

Queen's fifth album, it's title inspired by the Marx Brothers' film of the same name, was released in the UK on December 10 1976, going straight to Number One. The American release came eight days later and climbed to Number Five. In January 1977, the band flew to Boston Massachusetts for 10 days of rehearsals before embarking on a two month, 41 date tour of North America during which they began to experiment with moving and tilting light rigs.

They opened the shows with 'Tie Your Mother Down' which became their go-to song to either open or close gigs in the future. The band also adopted what would become the standard arrangement for 'Bohemian Rhapsody' on this tour – performing the first two verses on stage, then exiting and allowing the operatic section to be played over the PA system while dry ice and much lighting trickery evolved on the stage. Finally, Queen returned to play the hard rock section through to the end

Their support band on the USA leg of the tour were 'Boys Are Back In Town' rockers Thin Lizzy, fronted by Phil Lynott. In this, the year of Queen Elizabeth II's Silver Jubliee, the tour became known as the 'Queen Lizzy Tour'. Freddie Mercury's diva tendencies came to the fore during the Chicago gig. During the lengthy sound check, he refused to allow the audience – queueing in sub-zero temperatures outside – inside the venue. They were not amused, hence the egg throwing incident during their encore which in addition to inciting Freddie, caused Brian May to slip over. It was during 'The Day At The Races' tour that it dawned on May, Taylor and Deacon that Freddie was gay.

'We were touring in the States and suddenly he's got boys following him into his hotel room instead of girls,' Brian May recalled. 'We're thinking. . ."Mmmmm". That was really the extent of it. I always had plenty of gay friends, I just didn't realise that Freddie was one of them until later.'

Reviews of the tour were largely positive.

'The superb lighting, pyrotechnics and musical pulse from guitarist Brian May, bassist John Dean and drummer Roger Taylor have stayed at the same level since they departed the states last year,' wrote a journalist in the New York Times. 'It's one of the best integrated, most fully developed power trio sounds remaining today and without a lot of noise to mimic the real music. Deacon and Taylor remain visually unobtrusive but run together with May like finely-lubed cogs; and May's royal leads constantly tug the show to new levels. Queen know their own dynamics and their audience's inter-dynamics as well. Their pacing has become exquisite.'

Queen played the legendary Madison Square Garden for the first time on this tour – selling the venue out. Two sell-out nights at the Forum in Los Angeles followed. Although Thin Lizzy gave Queen a run for their money on occasion, there was no way they blew the regal combo off stage.

'However good Thin Lizzy were, once Queen came on with the full production, they wiped the floor with us most nights,' said Lizzy's tour manager at the time.

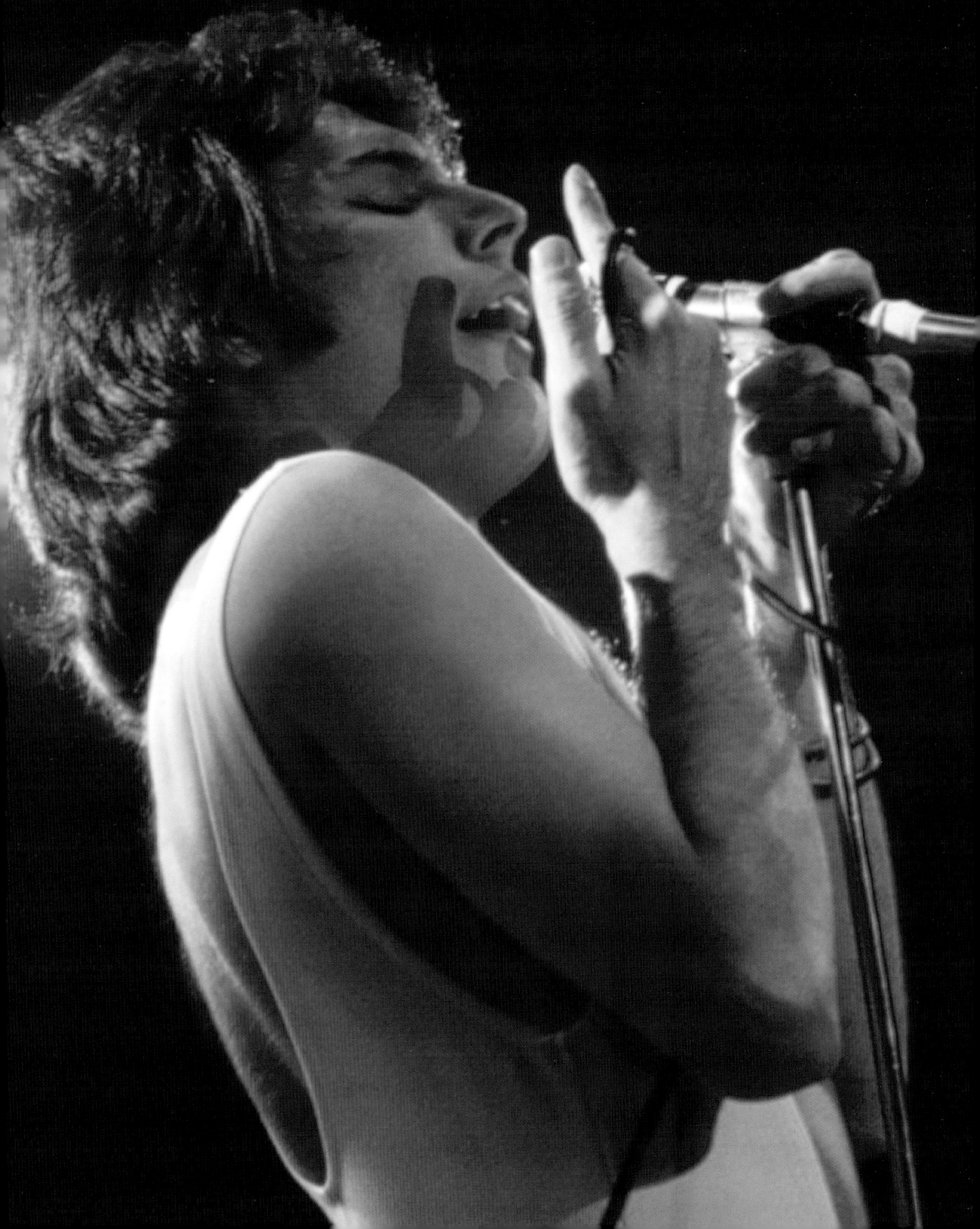

In April, quiet man bassist John Deacon wrote the quarterly fan club newsletter in which he looked back on the tour...

'We covered the whole of the US this time and did quite a few shows in Canada, too,' he wrote. 'It was the first time we had played in very large auditoriums like Los Angeles Forum and Madison Square Garden. It was very exciting for us to play to 20,000 at one concert. Our show went over very well in those auditoriums and the American crowds wouldn't let us go until we had done two or even three encores. As you probably know by now, we are doing a UK and European tour soon which we're really looking forward to as we haven't done a concert tour of England since November '75 and we haven't played in Europe for over two years.'

Opening the European tour in Stockholm, Sweden in May 1977, Freddie Mercury pulled out all the sartorial stage-wear stops. He came on stage in a replica of the second-skin like, harlequin-styled costume worn by the Russian ballet dancer Nijinsky, then took the final encore in an equally tight silver leotard, so heavily sequinned the audience were almost blinded when powerful spotlights bounced off the fabric. The dates on continental Europe successfully completed without incident, Queen set out on the road on home turf.

It was during the gig in Bingley, Staffordshire that Brian May first realised that the audience were virtually word-perfect with every song.

'When people started singing along, we found it kind of annoying,' he recalled. 'It was an enormous realisation. They sang every note of every song. Freddie and I looked at each other and went, "Something's happening here. We've been fighting it, and we should be embracing it". That's where "We Will Rock You" and "We Are the Champions" came from. It was an epoch-making moment.'

As were their two nights at Earls Court in London. Both shows were recorded – although these recordings have never been officially released. For these dates, Queen used a brand new, specially commissioned £50,000 lighting rig, referred to as 'The Crown'. Weighing almost nine-and-a-half tons and measuring 20 feet high, 45 feet deep and 54 feet wide, it ascended dramatically to illuminate a stage writhed in dry ice. The 17,000 capacity crowds on both nights loved the spectacle, enhanced by Mercury in his quick-silvery, jewelled leotard, and an ethereal-looking May in his white pleated cape. But the critics weren't impressed, not with pared-back and often brutal Punk Rock being at its height.

'A Rock gig is no longer the ceremonial idolisation of a star by fans,' read one NME review. 'That whole illusion, still perpetuated by Queen, is quickly being destroyed and in the iconoclastic atmosphere of the New Wave there is nothing more redundant than a posturing old ballerina toasting his audience with champagne.'

Mercury, however, remained defiant.

'The bigger the better,' he vowed. 'In everything.'

Madison Square Garden in New York City in February 1977

7 | News of the World Tour

'Freddie and I both thought it would be an interesting experiment to write a song with audience participation specifically in mind'

Brian May on how live anthem 'We Will Rock You' came about

1977

North America

Nov 11, Cumberland County Civic Center, Portland, Maine
Nov 12, Boston Gardens, Boston, Massachusetts
Nov 13, Civic Center, Springfield, Massachusetts
Nov 15, Civic Center, Providence, Rhode Island
Nov 16, Memorial Coliseum, New Haven, Connecticut
Nov 18/19, Cobo Hall, Detroit, Michigan
Nov 21, Maple Leaf Garden, Toronto, Ontario
Nov 23/24, The Spectrum, Philadelphia, Pennsylvannia
Nov 25, Scope Arena, Norfolk, Virginia
Nov 27, Richfield Coliseum, Cleveland, Ohio
Nov 29, Capitol Center, Washington DC
Dec 1-2, Madison Square Garden, New York
Dec 4, University Arena, Dayton, Ohio
Dec 5, Chicago Stadium, Chicago, Illinois
Dec 8, The Omni, Atlanta, Georgia
Dec 11, Tarrant County Convention Center, Fort Worth, Texas
Dec 14, Aladdin Center, Las Vegas, Nevada
Dec 16, Sports Arena, San Diego
Dec 17, County Coliseum, Oakland, California
Dec 20/21, Long Beach Arena, Long Beach, California
Dec 22, Inglewood Forum, Los Angeles

1978

Europe and UK

Apr 12, Ice Stadium Stockholm, Sweden
Apr 13, Falkoner Theatre, Copenhagen, Denmark
Apr 14, Ernst Merck Halle, Hamburg, Germany
Apr 16/17, Foret Nationale, Brussels, Belgium
Apr 19/20, Ahoy Hall, Rotterdam
Apr 21, Foret Nationale, Brussels, Belgium
Apr 23/24, Pavillion de Paris, Paris, France
Apr 26, Westfallenhalle, Dortmund, Germany
Apr 28, Deutschlandhalle, Berlin, Germany
Apr 30, Hallenstadion, Zurich, Switzerland
May 2, Stadhalle, Vienna, Austria
May 3, Olympiahalle, Munich, Germany
May 6/7, Bingley Hall, Stafford
May 11/12/13, Empire Pool, London

Mittwoch, 3. 5. 78
Beginn: 20.00 Uhr
Einlaß: 19.00 Uhr

presents
A Night With
QUEEN
Concert '78

23

Cooperation:
**Stimmen der Welt
& Lippmann + Rau**

Olympiahalle
München
Olympiapark

Tribüne	Block	Reihe	Sitz
	D 4	**19**	**5**

Verbill. Vorverkauf:	Abendkasse:
DM 18,00	**DM 21,00**
incl. 6 % MWSt. zuzügl. Vorverk.-Geb.	incl. 6 % MWSt.

Das Mitnehm. von Tonbandgeräten in d. Halle bzw. das Mitschneiden u. Filmen der Veranstaltung ist grundsätzl. verboten. Bei Zuwiderhandlung Verweis aus der Halle. Keine Haftung für Sach- u. Körperschäden. In keinem Fall Rückerstattung des Kaufpreises. Bei Verlassen der Halle verliert die Karte Gültigkeit.

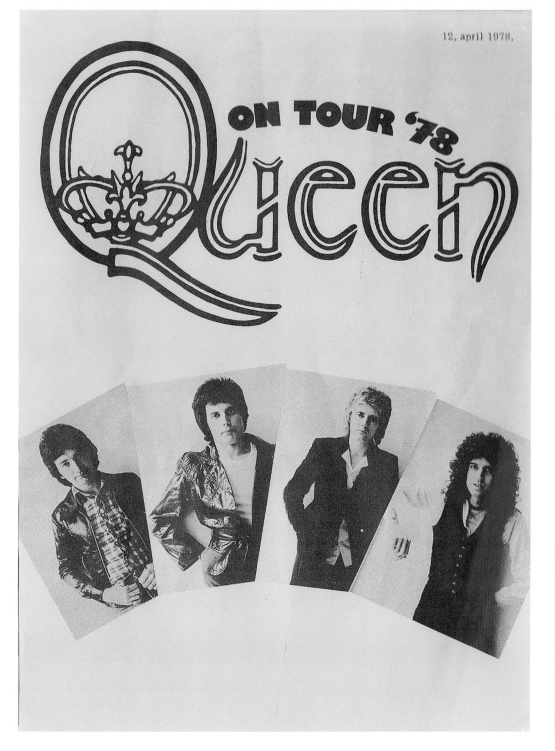

12. april 1978.

ON TOUR '78
Queen

Having recorded their sixth album 'News of the World' in just a couple of months, by November 1977, Queen were following what had become their regular album/tour/album/tour routine and were back out on the road. North America was their primary destination where the new album would climb to Number Three in the charts – their highest yet. 'We Will Rock You' and 'We Are The Champions' were two of the stand-out tracks on the album and these anthems – their composition inspired by the band's live shows – were used as the first encore during this tour. 'We Will Rock You' also opened the shows. It was on this tour that 'I'm In Love With My Car', penned by and featuring Roger Taylor on lead vocals, was initially introduced to the set list. This was also the first time in which the heart-rendering 'Love of My Life' was performed live as a reworked acoustic version and, almost immediately, it became a highlight of the show. The fans often took control of the vocals while Mercury conducted the audience like a choir. To make way for the new material, most songs from the first two Queen albums were omitted.

The Queen roadshow had become a massive machine, touring with over 60 tons of equipment, including the 'Crown' lighting rig, which a Boston-based sail making company had been commissioned to re-design in order to make it easier to ship in and out of venues. The stage was made up of two catwalks plus two platforms above the PA system which enabled Mercury to move around wherever he chose. The frontman, who'd had a haircut and now included a leather biker's jacket in his array of stage gear, was as flamboyant as ever, described in the US press as 'obnoxious and joyously camp'. However, some critics didn't approve of the way he ended the shows with a cynical 'Thank-you. It's been a pleasure doing business with you.'

This tour was the first the band performed without a support act and is was also notable for featuring some of Queen's longest shows, generally lasting two hours per night – in contrast to previous tours, where the shows would last around 1 hour and 40 minutes. The shows in Boston and Inglewood were particularly lengthy performances, with the concert in Boston clocking in at 2 hours and 25 minutes, and the concert in Inglewood clocking in at 2 hours and 15 minutes, making them the second and third longest shows in Queen's live career. The show at the Summit in Houston, Texas, was filmed and is widely considered by fans to be one of the best performances ever captured on celluloid, although

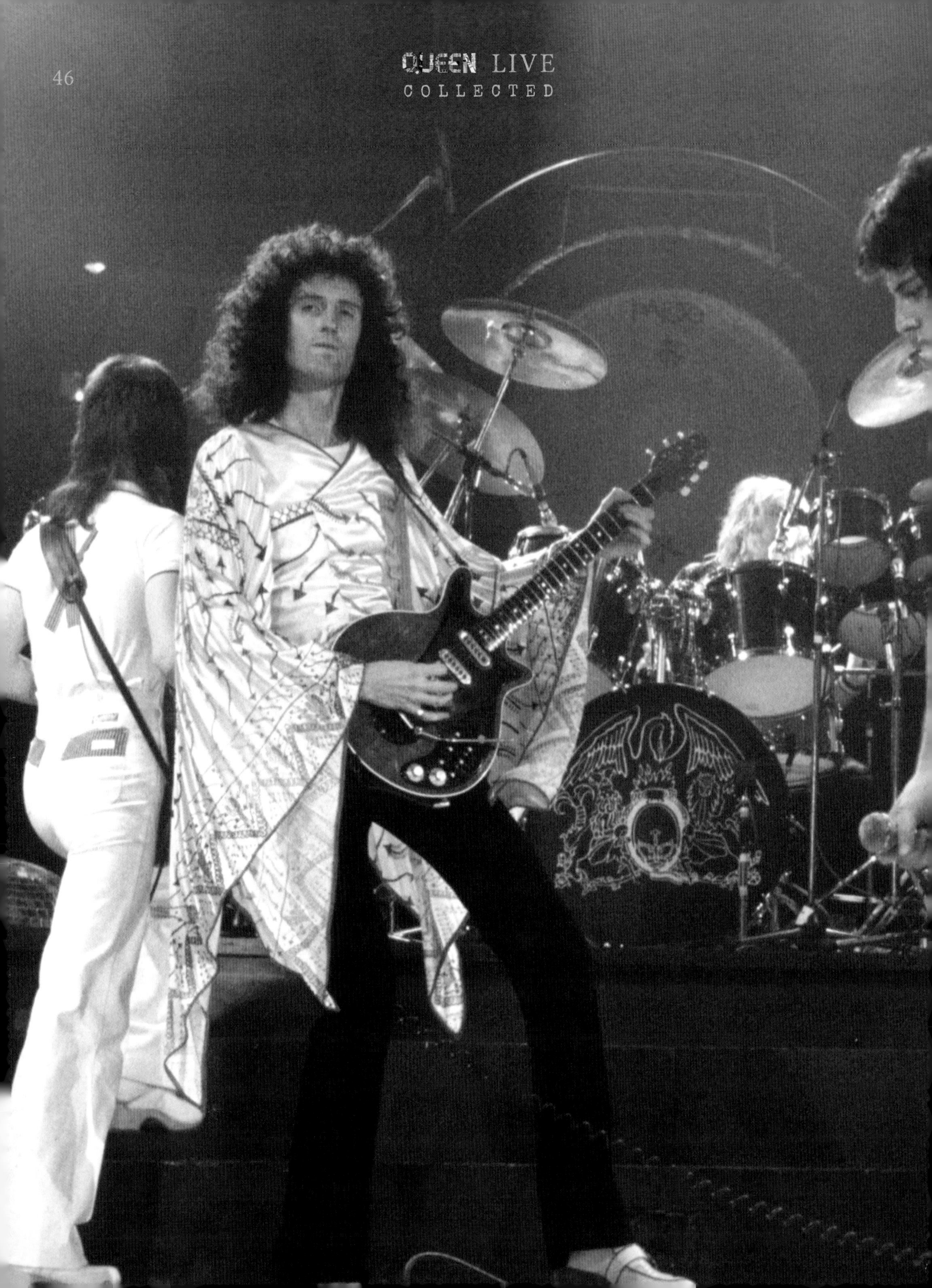

it has only ever been released as a bootleg.

Other stand-out dates on this tour included Queen's two nights at Madison Square Garden where Freddie reappeared for the first encore wearing a New York Yankees hat and jacket. The local baseball team had just claimed the sport's World Series and had adopted 'We Are The Champions' as their theme tune. In Portland, the audience completely took over the vocals on 'Love of My Life', leaving Freddie literally speechless. Mott's Ian Hunter saw the band perform in Toronto during which Brian May's amp exploded. The guitarist rushed over to tell Mercury who, seated at the piano, didn't know his microphone was switched on.

'Fred waved Brian away, saying, "Oh just jump around a bit and the silly bastards won't know the difference",' Hunter recalled. 'It was so funny.'

The final show of the tour in Los Angeles on December 22 was, unsurprisingly, as camp as Christmas. In a final encore, Queen's six feet, five inches' body guard took to the stage dressed as Santa Claus. On his back, he carried a huge sack from which a festively-themed Freddie emerged. Then a number of their entourage joined the band on stage dressed as Christmassy figures – reindeers, clowns, elves, of one whom was their manager, John Reid, gingerbread men and walking Christmas trees. Freddie and Brian played a version of 'White Christmas' and 5,000 balloons were released into the audience as mock snow and glitter was sprayed on stage. On Christmas Eve, the band flew back to the UK.

In April 1978 Queen embarked on a four-week European tour of 20 shows in nine countries. Freddie had started to change his look, and by the time the tour arrived in the UK for five dates that May, he had ditched the leotards for black PVC trousers, bare chest and braces. 'I rather fancy myself as a black panther,' he was quoted as saying. His second encore outfit was also altered – from a white sparkly spandex leotard to a red one with the arms and legs cut off. Brian May was still rocking his Rhodes drapes, Taylor his baggy shirts and Deacon his usual suit-like combo – shirt, trousers and waistcoat.

Accomodating 'The Crown' in some of the smaller venues proved to be a headache. In Hamburg and Copenhagen, for instance, the theatre ceilings were not sufficiently lofty to house the full rig and subsequently just the base lights were used. The Foret Nationale in Brussels, Belgium

Typical Set List

We Will Rock You
Brighton Rock
Somebody To Love
Death on Two Legs
Killer Queen
Good Old-Fashioned Lover Boy
I'm In Love With My Car
Get Down Make Love
Millionaire Waltz
You're My Best Friend
Spread Your Wings
Liar
Love Of My Life
39
My Melancholy Blues
White Man
Instrumental Inferno
The Prophet's Song (reprise)
Now I'm Here
Stone Cold Crazy
Bohemian Rhapsody
Tie Your Mother Down
We Will Rock You
We Are The Champions
Sheer Heart Attack
Jailhouse Rock
God Save The Queen

could accommodate the full majesty of 'The Crown' but there was a mechanical failure at the beginning of the show, and only one side rose.

'There was an explosion and loads of smoke,' recalled Brian May. 'One side of the crown majestically rose while the other majestically fell. I think it helped break the ice.'

Once the problem was rectified, the show was restarted.

For the first time in their career, Queen got to play Paris for two nights. Music journalist Tim Lott witnessed the second show, giving a colourful account of the evening's proceedings.

'Freddie Mercury appears on stage like a writhing python, stalking the boards in the black leotard he normally wears. Looking rather like an Edwardian one-piece bathing costume, scattered with large silver sequins, it reveals a thickly haired chest and a frame that doesn't carry an ounce of unnecessary flesh.

Before his entrance at the Pavillion de Paris a huge crown with flashing lights and steam shooting from its base, ascended from the stage. The young Parisian audience of 7000 plus were mesmerised as it settled into the roof of the concert hall.

Then as Queen broke into their first rousing number, "We Will Rock You", the audience rose to its feet, waving flame-darting cigarette lighters as a welcome to the four musicians. In the darkness of the vast stadium it was an incredible sight.

The concert, the first Queen had given in Paris during their six-year lifespan, was a triumph, with the French on their feet almost throughout the 2½ hour programme of intensive sound and light. Mercury, it seemed, had every justification for flippantly remarking afterwards: "Well, that's Paris ticked off".

Queen have become one of Britain's biggest exports. They have had six top selling LPs. Their last one, entitled "News of the World" sold over seven million copies worldwide, and the single "We Are The Champions" - a song adopted by football and rugby teams throughout America - has so far sold over five million.

For their American tour, which preceded the European engagements, they undertook 24 concert dates, and at the Forum, Los Angeles, they played to 64,000 people in three nights. Their present elaborate production set them back £55,000 and it costs £4000 a day to keep Queen's stage show on the road. Only in America do they come away with a profit, through being able to pack their audiences into 20,000 seater stadiums.

Musically the show I watched in Paris, which Queen are bringing to Wembley's Empire Pool for three nights from next Thursday, concentrates on their new album material, with songs "Get Down Make Love", "Spread Your Wings", "It's Late", "My Melancholy Blues", "We Are The Champions", and some familiar oldies thrown in like "Bohemian Rhapsody" and "Killer Queen".'

Before the Wembley dates, Queen rocked up to play two nights at Bingley Hall, Staffordshire. The atmosphere of the second date was vividly captured by the Birmingham Evening Mail.

'Their Highnesses deigned to give audience to their adoring subjects 35 minutes late. But what's that to the converted thousands, many of whom have been queueing since the previous day? Their arrival accompanied by the majestic music of the spheres and a fair representation of a spaceship take-off, transforms what should be a pop concert into more of a rock mass. The barn-like hall takes on the atmosphere of a cathedral. The regal quartet have style and swagger - and the skill to accompany it as they pulsate their way through their rhythmic hymnal. The show is ostentatious, exciting, and the only lull as they skip from heavy to light and fantastic, is during indulgent guitar and vocal solos which are electronic exercises rather than music. Quicksilver Freddie Mercury, in black plastic trousers and red braces makes "Bohemian Rhapsody" into something of a revelation.'

But this all would seem positively restrained in comparison with what was to come...

Freddie Mercury on stage, Deutschlandhalle, Berlin, 1978

8|Jazz Tour

'I thank you for your time and I thank you for your money'
Freddie Mercury's parting words to Queen's Madison Square Garden audience

1978

North America

Oct 28, Convention Center, Dallas, Texas
Oct 29, Mid South Coliseum, Memphis, Tennesse
Oct 31, St Bernard Civic Auditorium, New Orleans, Louisana
Nov 3, Sportatorium, Miami, Florida
Nov 4, Civic Centre, Lakeland, Florida
Nov 6, Capitol Centre, Washington DC
Nov 7, Coliseum, New Haven, Conneecticut
Nov 9/10, Cobo Arena, Detroit, Michigan
Nov 11, Wings Stadium, Kalamazoo, Michigan
Nov 13, Boston Gardens, Boston, Massachusetts
Nov 14, Rhode Island Civic Centre, Providence, Rhode Island
Nov 16/17, Madison Square Garden, New York
Nov 19, Coliseum, Nassau, Long Island
Nov 20, Spectrum, Philadelphia, Pennsylvania
Nov 22, Auditorium, Nashville, Tennessee
Nov 23, Checkerdome, St Louis, Missouri
Nov 25, Richfield Coliseum, Cleveland, Ohio
Nov 26, Riverfront Coliseum, Cincinatti, Ohio
Nov 28, War Memorial Auditorium, Buffalo, New York
Nov 30, Central Canadian Exhibition Centre, Ottawa, Ontario
Dec 1, The Forum, Montreal, Quebec
Dec 3/4 Maple Leaf Gardens, Toronto, Ontario
Dec 6, Dane County Coliseum, Madison, Wisconsin
Dec 7, Stadium, Chicago, Illinois
Dec 8, Kemper Arena, Kansas City, Missouri
Dec 12, Coliseum, Seattle, Washington
Dec 13, Coliseum, Portland, Oregon
Dec 14, PNE Coliseum, Vancouver, British Colombia
Dec 16, Coliseum, Oakland, California
Dec 18/19/20, Forum, Los Angeles

1979

Europe

Jan 17, Ernst Merck Halle, Hamburg. Germany
Jan 18, Ostseehalle, Kiel, Germany
Jan 20, Bremen Stadthalle, Bremen, Germany
Jan 21, Westfalenhallen Dortmund, Germany
Jan 23, Messesportspalace, Hanover, Germany
Jan 24, Deutschlandhalle, Berlin, Germany
Jan 26/27, Forest National, Brussels, Belgium
Jan 29/30, Ahoy Rotterdam, Holland
Feb 1, Sporthalle, Cologne, Germany
Feb 2, Frankfurt Festhalle, Frankfurt, Germany
Feb 4, Hallenstadion, Zurich, Switzerland
Feb 6, Dom Sportova, Zagreb, Yugoslavia
Feb 7, Hala Tivoli, Ljubljana, Yugoslavis
Feb 11, Rudi-Sedlmayer-Halle, Munich, Germany
Feb 13, Sporthalle, Stuttgart, Germany
Feb 15, Saarlandhalle, Saarbrücken, Germany
Feb 17, Palais des Sports de Gerland, Lyon, France
Feb 19/20/21, Palau dels Esports de Barcelona, Spain
Feb 23, Palacio de Deportes de la Comunidad, Madrid, Spain
Feb 25, Arenes de Poitiers, Poitiers, France
Feb 27/28 & March 1, Pavillon de Paris, Paris, France

Japan

Apr 13/14, Budokan, Tokyo
Apr 19/20, Osaka Festival Hall, Osaka
Apr 21, Jissen-rinri Memorial Hall, Kanazawa
Apr 23/24/25, Budokan, Tokyo

Typical Set List

We Will Rock You
Let Me Entertain You
Somebody To Love
If You Can't Beat Them
Death On Two Legs
Killer Queen
Bicycle Race
I'm In Love With My Car
Get Down Make Love
You're My Best Friend
Now I'm Here
Spread Your Wings
Dreamers Ball
Love Of My Life
39
It's Late
Brighton Rock
Fat Bottomed Girls
Keep Yourself Alive
Bohemian Rhapsody
Tie Your Mother Down
Sheer Heart Attack
We Will Rock You
We Are The Champions
God Save The Queen

Apr 27, Kobe Central Gymnasium
Apr 28, Nagoya International Display
Apr 30/May 1, Kyuden Memorial Gymnasium, Fukuoka
May 2, Prefectural Athletic Association, Yamaguchi
May 5, Makomanai Ice Arena, Sapporo

Plus
Aug 18, Ludwigsparkstadion, Saarbrücken Germany

Fritz Rau + Michael Scheller present

IN CONCERT

QUEEN

Freitag, 2. Feb. '79, 20 Uhr
Frankfurt · Festhalle

Innenraum: DM 22,–

zuzügl. Vorverkaufsgebühr inkl. 6 % MWSt.

№ 221

Tourneeleitung: Lippmann + Rau GmbH + Co. KG

Keine Haftung für Sach- und Körperschäden. Zurück mit nur bei
Absage oder Verlegung. Das Mitnehmen von Flaschen und Tonbandgeräten ist nicht erlaubt. Ton- und Filmaufnahmen auch für den
privaten Gebrauch – untersagt. Beim Verlassen der Halle verliert die
Karte ihre Gültigkeit. Mißbrauch wird strafrechtlich verfolgt.

CAPTURED... LIVE

QUEEN LIVE KILLERS

Late October 1978 saw Queen flying out to Dallas to prepare for a 35 date, seven-week tour of North America. The album 'Jazz' – recorded throughout summer and early autumn in France and Switzerland, and featuring songs 'Bicycle Race', 'Fat Bottomed Girls', 'Let Me Entertain You' and 'Don't Stop Me Now' – was officially launched at an outrageous party in New Orleans where transvestites, strippers dressed as nuns, fire-eaters, and dancing girls provided the entertainment. 'Jazz' made it to number two in the UK and six in the US. Four days before the tour began, 'Bicycle Race' and 'Fat Bottomed Girls' were issued in the US as a double A side.

The Jazz tour featured the new five ton 'Pizza Oven' lighting rig which consisted of 600 lights arranged on a massive moveable rig above the band. It was nicknamed the 'Pizza Oven' due to the massive amount of heat the red, white and green lights generated. Like 'The Crown', the new rig moved above the stage, facing out towards the audience when it reached the required height.

It wasn't only the lighting that had changed though. Freddie Mercury's look was no longer sequinned jumpsuits, skin-tight leotards or trousers. He'd gone full-on 'Gay Biker Clone' with leather biker cap, jacket and trousers, and heavy chain necklace. John Deacon, meanwhile, now sported a cropped haircut.

This tour was also the first to see and hear the now famous 'Brian-Brian' chant from the audience. Another unexpected feature of many shows were the requests for the seemingly inconspicuous song 'Mustapha'. On this tour, Mercury would sing only the opening few bars without accompaniment - as on the recorded version.

Freddie's voice and throat, however, were again giving him problems. He blamed his nodules but others felt his increasingly debauched lifestyle didn't helped.

'Around 1978 and 1979, when Queen became huge, Freddie's appetites soared,' a former road manager was later to say. 'He was non-stop sex and drugs. Before a show, after a show. . . Even between songs. Before an encore, he'd nip backstage, have a few lines of coke, get a quick blow job from some bloke he'd just met, then run back to the stage and finish the gig.'

To some observers, there seemed to be a 'sex theme' deliberately integrated into the shows. At Madison Square Garden the band, as they performed 'Fat Bottomed Girls', were joined onstage by nine topless female cyclists wearing just tiny G-strings and enthusiastically ringing their bicycle bells. The poster of nude ladies cycling around a UK stadium had not been included in the American release of 'Jazz '– as it had in the UK – so Queen had decided to treat their New York audience the real deal.

Some members of the American press were not impressed, one publication writing, 'How far will Queen go to keep people from noticing that it's not only the bicycle beauties that are bare?'

Others were more complimentary.

'They treated their listeners to songs off the new album "Jazz",' explained the Brooklyn College Kingsmen. 'Fat Bottomed Girl was performed as girls, adequately described by the song's title, rode across the stage in outfits quite risqué as the male populace seated in the upper promenades frantically reached for the binoculars. . . Mercury bowed and gestured to the audience as he emphasised the lyrics in "We Are The Champions" – "You've brought me fame and fortune and everything that goes with it – I thank you all" . . . As the final notes from Brian May's guitar echoed throughout the Garden after the band's third and final encore, fearless Freddie sauntered to the front of the stage, bowed graciously and said brashly, "I thank you for your time and I thank you for your money".'

Christmas 1978 in the UK and Queen announced their intention to perform a concert at Centre Court, Wimbledon the following year. Unsurprisingly the All England club turned down the request. In January, they set out on their biggest European tour to date - 28 shows in seven countries over a six-week period which would include their first shows in the then Yugoslavia.

'Don't Stop Me Now' featured on the set list for the first time and

Freddie Mercury & Brian May, Madison Square Garden

audiences the continent over were wowed by Roger Taylor's sonically powerful beats and backing vocals. During the Paris shows, Freddie Mercury noticed that the same faces were at the front of the audience as had been on several occasions before. He referred to them as 'The Royal Family' and the tag stuck. This 'Family' were mainly British fans who made a point of following the band around Europe. It was while they were in Paris that they each brought a bicycle bell to the gig which, to the delight of Queen, they rang in unison as the appropriate moment during 'Bicycle Race'. The next night, French fans followed suite with the result that hundreds of bike bells were rung at the same time!

In April '79, Queen set off for Japan where they would perform 17 shows – their largest tour ever in the Land of the Rising Sun. To

Ahoy, Rotterdam, Netherlands, 29th January 1979

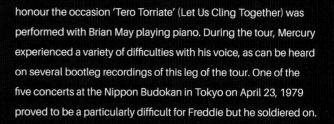

honour the occasion 'Tero Torriate' (Let Us Cling Together) was performed with Brian May playing piano. During the tour, Mercury experienced a variety of difficulties with his voice, as can be heard on several bootleg recordings of this leg of the tour. One of the five concerts at the Nippon Budokan in Tokyo on April 23, 1979 proved to be a particularly difficult for Freddie but he soldiered on.

Two months later, EMI released Queen's first live album, entitled 'Live Killers', made up of various recordings from the band's Jazz tour dates in Europe. A live album had been mooted since the 1974 gig at London's Rainbow Theatre but there were concerns that a live recording would never stand up next to Queen's perfectly produced studio albums which, in all honesty, it did not. But in addition to generating extra sales, the band wanted to try and stop the proliferation of bootlegs.

'Live albums are inescapable really,' commented Brian May. 'Everyone tells you you have to do them and when you do, you find that they're often not of mass appeal, and in the absence of a fluke condition, you sell your album to the converted – the people who know your stuff and already come to your concerts.'

In August 1979, Queen headlined the Saarbruken Festival in Germany. Others bands on the bill included Ten Years After, Rory Gallagher, Molly Hatchet and the Commodores. The decision to perform there was an attempt to boost the band's profile in the country. Playing before a capacity crowd of 30,000, it was mainly memorable for Roger Taylor's bright green hair following a failed attempt at dyeing his locks earlier in the day! He was later to say it was one of the most mortifying experiences of his life – not helped by the fact that Freddie took every opportunity he could to laugh at him on stage. It's said that Taylor was so incensed by what had happened, he tracked down every photograph that had been taken and had them all destroyed. It's also rumoured that he demolished his drum-kit after the gig, feeling that technical problems had ruined his performance.

9|Crazy Tour

'It's nice to be somewhere where people can actually see and hear y

Brian May's verdict on The Crazy Tour's smaller venues

1979

UK

Nov 22, Royal Society Hall, Dublin, Ireland

Nov 24, National Exhibition Centre, Birmingham

Nov 26/7, Apollo Theatre, Manchester

November 30/December 1, Apollo Theatre, Glasgow

Dec 3/4 City Hall, Newcastle-upon-Tyne

Dec 6/7, Empire Theatre, Liverpool

Dec 9, Hippodrome, Bristol

Dec 10/11, Brighton Centre, Brighton

Dec 13, Lyceum Ballroom, London

Dec 14, Rainbow Theatre, London

Dec 17, Tiffany's, Purley, London

Dec 19, Tottenham Mayfair, London

Dec 20, Lewisham Odeon, London

Dec 22, Alexandra Palace, London

Dec 26, Hammersmith Odeon, London

THE BRIGHTON CENTRE

MONDAY, 3rd DEC., 1979 at 8.00 p.m.

HARVEY GOLDSMITH present **QUEEN** in CONCERT

STANDING TICKET
MAIN HALL ONLY £5.00

BRIGHTON CENTRE RESTAURANT
(Magnificent Sea View)
Open two hours prior to most performances
Reservations: Telephone 203130

Neither the Council or their officers accept any responsibility for any loss or damage (howsoever caused or sustained) to any property whatsoever brought on to these premises.

Tickets cannot be exchanged or refunded.

The taking of unauthorised photographs during an artiste's live performance is a breach of the Copyright Act 1956. Cameras being used in defiance of this regulation will be removed to the cloakroom for the duration of the performance. The Management may also exercise the right to expose film if so requested by the artiste.

Typical Set List

Intro

We Will Rock You

Let Me Entertain You

Somebody to Love

Mustapha

Death On Two Legs

Killer Queen

I'm In Love With My Car

Get Down Make Love

You're My Best Friend

Save Me

Now I'm Here

Don't Stop Me Now

Love Of My Life

39

Keep Yourself Alive

Brighton Rock

Crazy Little Thing Called Love

Bohemian Rhapsody

Tie Your Mother Down

Sheer Heart Attack

We Are The Champions

We Will Rock You

God Save The Queen

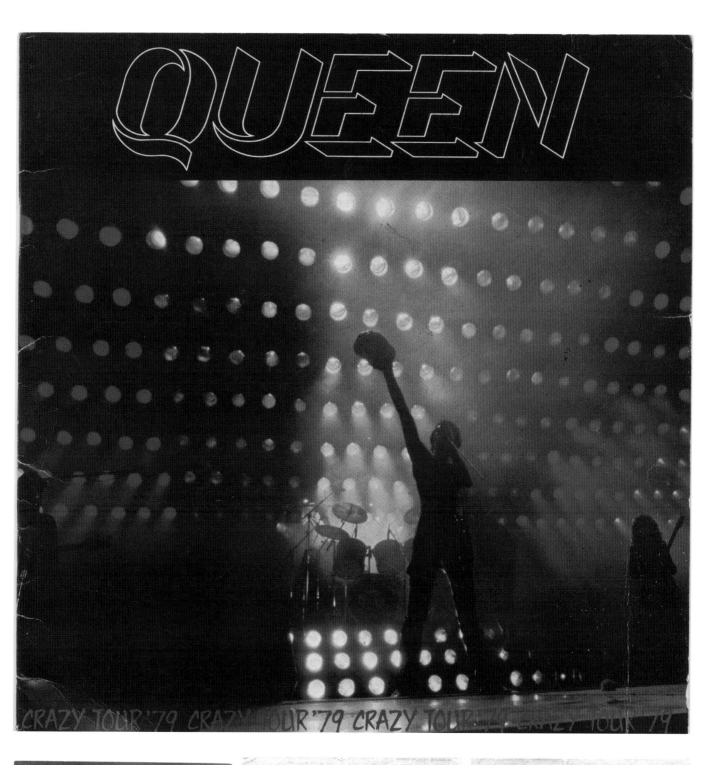

CRAZY TOUR '79 CRAZY TOUR '79 CRAZY TOUR '79 CRAZY TOUR '79

EMPIRE THEATRE
Liverpool

Harvey Goldsmith presents—

Queen

Thursday, 6th December 1979

Evening 7.30 p.m.

FRONT STALLS
£4.75

G 16 1

ABC Printers, Manchester

THIS PORTION TO BE RETAINED

EMPIRE THEATRE
Liverpool

Harvey Goldsmith presents—

Queen

Friday, 7th December 1979

Evening 7.30 p.m.

CENTRE STALLS ⑦
£4.75

P 12 2

ABC Printers, Manchester

THIS PORTION TO BE RETAINED

APOLLO THEATRE
ARDWICK, MANCHESTER

Harvey Goldsmith Enterprises present -

Queen

Monday, 26th November 1979

Evening 7.30 p.m.

REAR CIRCLE
£4.00

P 2

ABC Printers, Manchester

RETAIN THIS PORTION

1

No Cameras or Recording Equipment
Official Programmes sold in the Theatre.
No Ticket exchanges or money refunds.

QUEEN

UNICEF and the UNITED NATIONS HIGH COMMISSIONER
FOR REFUGEES proudly presents

UNICEF

CONCERTS FOR THE PEOPLE OF KAMPUCHEA

at the Hammersmith Odeon

Wednesday 26th December
to
Saturday 29th December

Minimum Contribution £1.00

The down-sized Crazy Tour in late 1979 was preceded by a single release – 'Crazy Little Thing Called Love' – rather than a new album. In the UK, the track reached number two in the charts but gave Queen their first, long-awaited number one single in the US. But instead of touring North America again, the band decided to scale back and embark on playing 20 dates at smallish venues around the UK.

'We'd been accused of being too grand,' said Roger Taylor. 'So, this was our way of getting closer to the audience, and to prove to the critics, "F**k you, we can go down just as well in a 1400 seater". It became known as the "Crazy" tour because of the fact that we were crazy for doing it. It was "crazy" as in we could have done a couple of nights at Wembley instead.'

Venues included the decidedly snug Tiffany's in Purley, The Mayfair in Tottenham and The Lewisham Odeon. The tour began in Dublin – the first time the band had played in Ireland – where they performed a specially rehearsed version of 'Danny Boy'. Out of respect, they chose not to close the show with 'God Save The Queen'.

On stage, Brian May and Roger Taylor looked much the same as ever. John Deacon, however, opted for a conservative collar and tie while Freddie was never out of leathers – although he did wear one red knee pad and one blue one at the Liverpool gig in order to please the supporters of the city's respective football teams. In some concerts, Mercury would appear on stage near the closing of the show sitting on the shoulders of a crew member dressed as Superman or Darth Vader, although this led to some minor legality problems.

The largest audience Queen played to was 14,000 at Birmingham's National Exhibition Centre where, during 'Don't Stop Me Now', the ubiquitous Royal Family fans did a conga at the back of the hall with security staff joining in.

'Queen got a right royal reception from 14,000 fans at the NEC,' proclaimed the Birmingham Evening Mail. 'The stars of the show were in impressive form. The range of versatility that has elevated Queen to super-group status was all there.'

Even the usually dismissive members of the music press were impressed – in spite of themselves.

'The ULTIMATE rock show!' extolled Sounds music paper. 'Glittering and glorious. A music form that has long reached its peak. I hate good/bad old rock music, but even I can enjoy cricket when it's played properly. The music of Queen pours from the sky and unless you are equipped with suitable weather-wear, you are going to get wet. I was drenched. I have never felt the slightest desire to listen to a Queen album since the heady days of 'Night at the Opera'. The string of awful (albeit cleverly awful) singles have succeeded only in transforming my lack of desire into a snobbish lack of respect. Do you catch my drift? You are anticipating another hatchet job, right? You are wrong. Y'see, I really hated Queen until. . .8.45 Monday evening when rock band Queen ceremoniously exploded into life on the Manchester Apollo Stage. Freddie Mercury bobbed charismatically into the centre of the crowd's attention – a confusing mass of flashing lights and pounding opening chords turned the initial tenseness into a staggering spectacle. Queen played with courage, and to my utter surprise, total conviction. I never imagined for one moment that they could be THIS good. The show (for it was a show rather than a gig) continued to impress me with its professional ferocity. Dozens of familiar and meaningless songs seemed to change into enjoyable tunes packed with humour. A humour that was never apparent to me before. . . I left the Apollo in a state of absolute amazement. The realisation that I'd actually enjoyed every second of a credibility-blowing Queen gig was beginning to burn away at my confused mind. There is no hope for me now.'

For Brian May, in particular, playing these smaller venues was a joy.

'Unless people can see you in their home town, it can almost

Munich Olypiahalle on November 02, 1979

seem like you don't exist,' he said. 'It's nice to be somewhere where people can actually see and hear you. The advantage of what we're doing is that because our sound and lighting systems are better than ever, we can really knock audiences in the stomach.'

However, their bulky lighting rig was problematic. They had down-sized 'The Pizza Oven' but even so, it was still too large to fit into the 2000 seater Lyceum Theatre in London.

'The roof was too small to fit all our lights,' Roger Taylor explained. 'So, we asked the manager if it would be OK to drill two holes in it. He was fine about it so long as we paid for the holes. Then we got a call from Paul McCartney saying that Wings were playing there the next week, and that they'd need a hole in the roof, too, so could he pay for one of them? We became the first ever group to sell Paul McCartney a hole!'

This was not to be the only Macca connection. The former Beatle contacted Queen to ask them to play at the Hammersmith Odeon on December 26 as part of the Concert for Kampuchea (now Cambodia). Showing no signs of exhaustion, Queen played a full set regarded as one of the best shows of the year. Freddie's voice was back to its soaring best and he therefore dared to be very experimental. He wasn't afraid to try reaching the high notes, some of which he had never attempted in a live setting before, in 'Bohemian Rhapsody' and 'We Are the Champions'. Finally, Fred let rip during 'Sheer Heart Attack' by trashing the monitors before reappearing on Superman's shoulders.

It was an incredible way for the band to end the '70s – a decade which had seen them go from obscurity to total super stardom. What would the 1980s bring?

10|The Game Tour

'People are giving you two hours of their time, so you have to give them everything for those two hours. We want every person to go away feeling he got his money's worth, and we use every possible device to achieve that'

Brian May

1980

North America

Jun 30, PNE Coliseum, Vancover, British Colombia
Jul 1, Coliseum, Seattle, Washington
Jul 2, Coliseum, Portland, Oregon
Jul 5, Sports Arena, San Diego
Jul 6, Compton Terrace, Arizona
Jul 8/9/11/12, The Forum, Los Angeles
Jul 13/14, Coliseum, Oakland, California
Aug 5, Mid South Coliseum, Memphis, Tennessee
Aug 6, Riverside Centroplex, Baton Rouge, Louisiana
Aug 8, City Myriad, Oklahoma City
Aug 9, Reunion, Dallas, Texas
Aug 10, Summit, Houston, Texas
Aug 12, The Omni, Atlanta, Georgia
Aug 13, Charlotte Coliseum, North Carolina
Aug 14, Greensboro Coliseum, North Carolina
Aug 16, Civic Center, Charleston, South Carolina
Aug 17, Riverton Coliseum, Cincinnati, Ohio
Aug 20, Civic Center, Hartford, Connecticut
Aug 22, Spectrum, Philadelphi, Pennsylvania
Aug 23, Civic Center, Baltimore, Maryland
Aug 24, Civic Center, Pittsburgh, Pennsylvania
Aug 26, Civic Center, Providence, Rhode Island
Aug 27, Spectrum, Portland, Maine
Aug 29, The Forum, Montreal, Quebec
Aug 30, GNE Grandstand, Toronto, Ontario
Sep 10, Mecca, Milwaukee, Wisconsin
Sep 11, Market Square Arena, Indianpolis, Indiana

Sep 12, Civic Center, Omaha, Nebraska
Sep 14, St Paul Civic Center, Minneapolis, Minnesota
Sep 16, Kemper Arena, Kansas City, Missouri
Sep 17, Checkerdome, St Louis, Missouri
Sep 19, Horizon, Chicago, Illinois
Sep 20, Joe Louis Arena, Detroit, Michigan
Sep 21, Cleveland Coliseum, Cleveland, Ohio
Sep 23, Veterans Memorial Coliseum, New Haven, Connecticut
Sep 24, War Memorial, Syracuse, New York
Sep 26, Boston Gardens, Boston, Massachusets
Sep 28/29/30 & October 1, Madison Square Garden, New York

Europe

Nov 23, Hallenstadion, Zurich, Switzerland
Nov 25, Le Bourget, La Retonde, Paris, France
Nov 26, Sportshalle, Cologne, Germany
Nov 27, Gornoordhalle, Leiden, Germany
Nov 29, Grundhalle, Essen, Germany
Nov 30, Deutschlanhalle, Germany
Dec 1, Stadthalle, Bremen, Germany
Dec 5/6, NEC, Birmingham, UK
Dec 8/9/10, Wembley Arena, London, UK
Dec 12/13, Foret Nationale, Brussels, Belgium
Dec 14, Festhalle, Frankfurt, Germany
Dec 16, Hall Rheus, Strasbourg, France
Dec 18, Olympiahalle, Munich, Germany

BIRMINGHAM INTERNATIONAL ARENA
NATIONAL EXHIBITION CENTRE

HARVEY GOLDSMITH ENTERTAINMENTS
present

QUEEN
IN CONCERT
in the new
Birmingham International Arena

SATURDAY, 6th DECEMBER, 1980,
at 8.00 p.m. *Doors open 6.30 p.m.*

£5.50
inc. VAT

No cameras, tape
recorders or bottles
allowed in Auditorium.

WARNING : Official
souvenirs are on
sale within the
Auditorium only.

For conditions
see over.

BLOCK
B

ROW
Y

SEAT

5

TO BE RETAINED

QUEEN IN CONCERT
AT THE SUMMIT

SUN. AUG. 10,1980 8:00PM
.65 PARKING FEE INCLUDED

UPPER PROM.   ADULT
212   A   9   9.65
    sec/box   row   seat   tax included

1981

Japan

Feb 12/13/16/17/18, Budokan Hall, Tokyo

South America

aka Gluttons for Punishment Tour

First Leg

Feb 28/March 1, Velez Sarfield, Buenos Aires, Argentina
Mar 4, Estadio Municipal, Mar Del Plata, Argentina
Mar 6, Alletico Rosario Central, Rosario, Argentina
Mar 20/21, Morumbi Stadium, Sao Paulo, Brazil

Second Leg

Sep 25/26/27, Poliedro De Caracas, Caracas, Venezuela
Oct 9, Estadion Universitano, Monterey, Mexico
Oct 16/17, Estadion Cuahtermoc, Puebla, Mexico

Plus

November 24/25, Forum, Montreal, Quebec

Typical Set List

Intro
Jailhouse Rock
We Will Rock You
Let Me Entertain You
Play The Game
Mustapha
Death On Two Legs
Killer Queen
I'm In Love With My Car
Get Down Make Love
Save Me
Now I'm Here
Dragon Attack
Now I'm Here (reprise)
Fat Bottomed Girls
Love Of My Life
Keep Yourself Alive
Brighton Rock
Crazy Little Thing called Love
Bohemian Rhapsody
Tie Your Mother Down
Another One Bites The Dust
Sheer Heart Attack
We Will Rock You
We Are The Champions
God Save The Queen

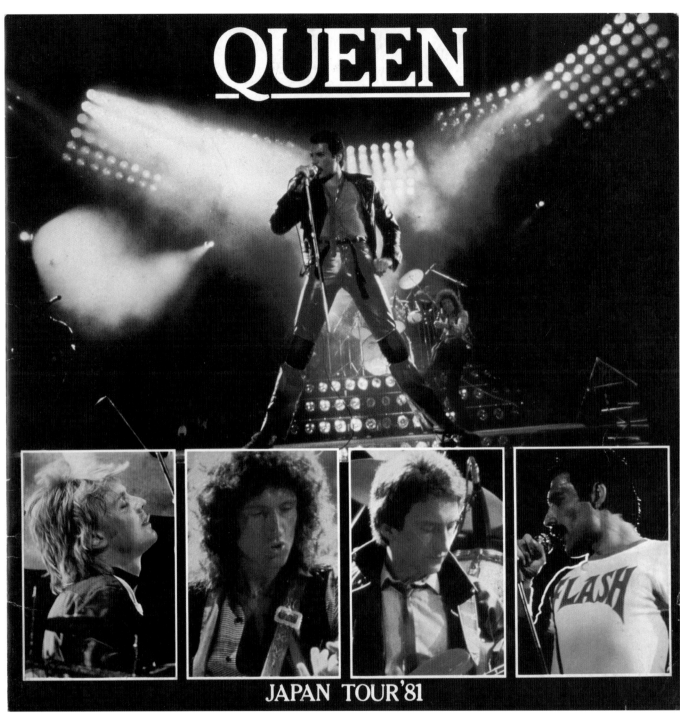

QUEEN

JAPAN TOUR '81

02017

SEC ROW SEAT

GEN. ADM.

SEPT 13, 1980

ADMIT ONE THIS DATE ONLY

NO EXCHANGE

CONCERTS WEST
Presents

QUEEN
CIVIC AUDITORIUM ARENA

SEPT **13** 1980

OMAHA, NEBRASKA

SATURDAY
8:00 P.M.

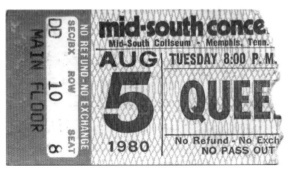

SEC/BX ROW SEAT

DD 10 8

MAIN FLOOR

NO REFUND - NO EXCHANGE

mid-south conce
Mid-South Coliseum - Memphis, Tenn.

AUG TUESDAY 8:00 P.M.

5 QUE

1980

No Refund - No Exch
NO PASS OUT

QUEEN
JAPAN TOUR '81

日本武道館大ホール　　2月16日(月)　開場PM5:30　主催/渡辺エンタープライズ・渡辺プロダクション
　　　　　　　　　　　　　　　　　　　　　　　開演PM6:30　協力/ワーナー・パイオニア

S ¥4,000 北 1 階 E 列 16 番

QUEEN
8:00PM FRI AUG 22 1980
Spectrum
NO REFUNDS/EXCHANGES
31604094BX5256

922 1LEV1
8:00P F
F 3 5
$9.05 3
0.45TAX
$9.50 5

SEAT ROW

THE CENTER GLENS FALLS NY
ONE CIVIC CENTER PLAZA
WQBK PRESENTS
QUEEN
NO REFUNDS/EXCH.
329455G8RM0422 09027/7
7:30P TUE SEP 23 1980

DATE/EVENT CODE
923 11FLOR
7:30P 106
106 Q 5
PRICE $9.50 Q
TOTAL $9.50 5

Montag, 1. Dezember '80 · 20 Uhr
Bremen · Stadthalle I

Mike Scheller Concerts presents

QUEEN
in Concert

№ 6516
Die Haftung für Sach- und Körperschäden. Zurücknahme nur bei
Absage oder Verlegung. Das Mitnehmen von Flaschen und Tonbandgeräten
ist nicht erlaubt. Ton- und Filmaufnahmen – auch für den privaten
Gebrauch – untersagt. Beim Verlassen der Halle verliert die Karte ihre
Gültigkeit. Mißbrauch wird strafrechtlich verfolgt.

LIONS CONCERTS n.v. - s.a. present
QUEEN
Vorst - Forest Nationa(a)l - Brussels
Vrijdag 12 december 1980 te 20 u.
Vendredi 12 décembre 1980 à 20 h.
400 Fr.
№ 07214
TICKETS VOET - 9800 DEINZE

WEMBLEY ARENA
HARVEY GOLDSMITH ENTERTAINMENTS
presents

WEDNESDAY, 10 DECEMBER, 1980
at 8 p.m.

ARENA

£6.00

TO BE RETAINED See conditions on back

DECEMBER
10
ENTER AT
NORTH DOOR
BLOCK
D
ROW
2
SEAT
13

DEUTSCHLANDHALLE
Messedamm 22, Autobus 4, 10, 65, 66, 64, 92, 94 U-Bahn Kaiserdamm (Kuhtränger) S-Bahn Ubbing

Sonntag, 30. November 1980　　Beginn siehe Rückseite

★　QUEEN IN CONCERT

DM 20,—
Tourneeleitung: Mike Scheller Concerts GmbH
Programmänderungen vorbehalten

Ort. Veranstalter: Concert Concept GmbH
Haftungsansprüche sowie Kartenrücknahme ausgeschlossen

Incl. 6,5% MwSt.
5285 ✳ Verbilligter Vorverkauf DM 20,—
+ Vorverkaufsgebühr

30. 11. 1980

Queen's ninth album, 'The Game', featuring hit singles 'Another One Bites the Dust' and 'Crazy Little Thing Called Love', was released in June 1980 and went to number one all over Europe. Ditto the US. They flew to LA on June 19 for a week of rehearsals before setting off on tour – a tour consisting of 46 shows over a three-month period and the biggest they'd ever undertaken. All the dates sold out. As the tour began, however, it was Freddie's droopy moustache that garnered most attention with disposable razors regularly being thrown on stage at some gigs.

'D'you girls like this moustache?' he'd tease from the stage between numbers. 'D'you boys like this moustache? A lot of people hate it. I don't give a f∗∗k!'

The facial hair wasn't the only change to Freddie's look. His stage gear seemed less flamboyant than in earlier outings. He now rocked T shirts and sports shoes rather than head-to-toe leather. There were technical changes to the show, too. Yet another new lighting rig, nicknamed 'The Fly Swatter' took pride of place. Made up of several moving arms covered in banks of lights, they rose up and around during the show. Roger Taylor, meanwhile, was the proud owner of a highly individual bass drum skin which was decorated with an image of his own face. 'Just in case he ever got amnesia, he'd know who he was,' quipped his drum roadie.

Six songs from 'The Game' were added to the set list that now opened with 'Jail House Rock'. 'Another One Bites The Dust' was only played sporadically. It was difficult, live, to get the same dry drum sound as on the album. Plus, not all the fans approved of its decidedly funky feel. 'They thought it not very rock and roll,' said Brian May who, if truth be told, was probably of the same opinion.

However, the John Deacon penned number with its hypnotic bass line became a smash hit around the world. It sold 4.5 million copies in the US alone and stayed at number one for five weeks.

Queen closed the North American leg of the tour by playing three nights at Madison Square Garden. So devoted were the audience, they didn't flinch when Freddie sprayed the front few rows with champagne and called them all 'c∗∗ts'!

'The Game' Europe commenced with six dates in Switzerland and Germany in November 1980. For the first encore in Zurich, Freddie sat on the shoulders of his burly body guard who was disguised as Darth Vader. The band also had a synthesizer on stage for the first time to enable them to play the medley from their new 'Flash Gordon' single.

Back on home turf, Queen headlined the NEC in Birmingham. The gig was reviewed by Melody Maker which read, 'As a guitarist, Brian May is superb, running the gamut of guitar virtuosity, utilising all manner of technical effects but never disguising his innate ability. . . As front man, ringmaster and manipulator, Mercury is incomparable. Exhorting, cajoling the audience, worshipped because of his inaccessibility, a perfect post Ziggy Stardust idol, remote and idolised. If that's how you like your heroes, then fine.'

It was at Birmingham that Freddie once again set out to shock by donning the tiniest pair of leather shorts imaginable for the encore. The crew placed bets on whether he'd split them or not. He didn't!

On December 8, 9 and 10, Queen played Wembley where, during the second gig, they performed a hastily rehearsed version of

Queen perform in concert at the Forum on July 9, 1980 in Inglewood, California

'Imagine' as a tribute to John Lennon who had been shot dead the day before. The band were big fans with Roger Taylor saying, 'John Lennon was my ultimate hero.'

Back in Germany for the final European dates, they played 'Imagine' for a second and last time at the Frankfurt gig, Queen returned to the UK for Christmas and New Year before flying out to Japan in February '81 where they would headline five nights at the Budokan before capacity audiences of 12,000 a night. New Romantic pop star Gary Numan, who happened to be in Tokyo, attended all three shows.

A week after leaving Japan, Queen were on their way to South America for their first tour on that continent. Dubbed 'The Gluttons for Punishment' tour, the trip had been in the planning stages for approximately nine months – it would be a prohibitively expensive to stage each show but as Freddie Mercury quipped, 'F**k the cost, darlings! Let's live a little.' The logistics were also the stuff of nightmares. Equipment hire was not available in South America at the time, with the result that 20 tons of sound gear had to be shipped in to the Velez Sarsfield football stadium in Buenos Aires from Japan. A further 40 tons were transported from Miami. In addition to sourcing equipment, it was the band's responsibility to provide 100 rolls of artificial turf to cover the football pitch.

'That was half the problem,' Brain May recalled. 'Trying to get permission for the audience to actually stand on the pitch.'

Queen were literally welcomed like royalty in Argentina with their music playing over the tannoy as they landed at the airport. Flanked by armed guards as they played their first gig at the Velez Sarsfield, the 54,000 strong crowd treated every song like an encore.

'Argentina had never seen anything like it,' wrote one fan. 'At the beginning, there was something like a UFO descend onto the stage. There were amazing lights, smoke. . . it was like magic. Everyone had goose pimples. People were literally sobbing all around.'

John Deacon, Brian May, Freddie Mercury and Roger Taylor of Queen perform on stage at Wembley Arena, on December 10th, 1980 in London

A review of the second night's show at the stadium, which was broadcast live on TV and watched by an astounding 35 million people in Argentina and Brazil, in the magazine 'Rolling Stone' read. . . ' "Un supergroupo numero uno" the MC announces as the lights dim, and with a burst of smoke, Queen appears on stage and begins hammering out its anthem We Will Rock You. Mercury – dressed in a white, sleeveless superman T shirt, red vinyl pants and a black vinyl jacket – frequently stops singing and dares the audience to carry the weight. And carry the weight, they do. The fans seem to know all the lyrics throughout the 110 minute show – which if for no other reason is impressive for the number of hits the group is able to offer such as Keep Yourself Alive, Killer Queen, Bohemian Rhapsody, Fat Bottomed Girls and Bicycle Race. Though the band interaction is remarkable, the crowd responds with such unquestioning devotion I get the feeling that if Freddie Mercury told them to shave their heads they'd do it. For the encore, the band reprises We Will Rock You then bounds into We Are The Champions. Mercury, by this time wearing only a pair of black leather shorts and a policeman's leather hat, struts around the stage, climatically kicking over a speaker cabinet and bashing it with his microphone stand. The kids love it!'

The band – even Freddie – were humbled by the reception they received.

'We really were nervous,' he said after the success of the first show. 'We had no right to automatically expect the works from an alien territory. I don't think they'd ever seen such an ambitious show, with this much lighting and effects.'

Ever-modest Brian May added, 'It's a long time since we've felt such warmth from a new audience, although we couldn't see much because of the size of the crowd. We feel really good about it now, as if our ambitions have been partly realised again.'

Following two further dates in Argentina, Queen moved on to Brazil – performing at Estádio do Morumbi in Sao to audiences of 131,000 and 120,000 on consecutive nights. It was here that one of the most moving moments in Queen's 'live' history happened, when 130,000 fans sang along to 'Love Of My Life' – a scene rec-

reated in the 2018 'Bohemian Rhapsody' biopic. At the time, few international bands viewed Brazil as an important tour destination, and the success of Queen's shows there helped cement the country as a must-stop for bands touring in South America.

The second leg of the South American tour, in September 1981, wasn't so successful. Queen experienced problems over cancelled gigs, security, corruption, unfit venues and out of control audiences.

In Venezuela, Queen played only three shows of the five planned as a period of national mourning was called after the death of former president Romulo Betancourt. In Mexico, they played three shows, one in Monterrey and two in Puebla, during which Mercury was said to have appeared wearing an oversized sombrero, prompting the crowd to throw shoes at the band, according to a witness in the audience. Afterward, Freddie left the stage, thanking the crowd for their shoes and called the crowd a 'bunch of tacos'. One of the Puebla gigs was even worse. The majority of the audience had been allowed into the stadium with ghetto blaster recorders in order to record the gig. When the batteries ran out, they began throwing them at the band – together with rocks and dirt. According to Queen's road manager, the crowd liked the band but with many off their faces on tequila and mescalin, they had just gone totally wild. Queen got to the end of the show but Freddie signed off by yelling, 'Adios amigos, you motherf∗∗kers.'

The band were desperate to leave but although their South and Central American experience ended badly, they'd created quite a legacy. Overall Queen played to approximately 700,000 people in the space of just 13 concerts with the show at Rio de Janeiro in Brazil setting the world record for the biggest paying audience. They also got to meet Argentinian footballing legend Maradona.

Queen's last live gigs of the year took place in Montreal, Canada on November 24 and 25. The shows were arranged because the band wanted to put together a full-length film in order to document their live show. The film, entitled, 'We Will Rock You,' was released on video in 1984 and showcases Queen at the very top of their game.

11|Hot Space Tour

'We hated each other for a while'

Brian May

1982

Europe

Apr 9, Scandinavium, Gothenburg, Sweden
Apr 10, Isstadion, Stockholm, Sweden
Apr 12, Drammenshallen, Oslo, Norway
Apr 16/17, Hallenstadion, Zurich, Switzerland
Apr 19/20, Palais de Sport, Paris, France
Apr 22/23, Foret Nationale, Brussels, Belgium
Apr 24/25, Groenoordhalle, Leiden, Holland
Apr 28/29, Festhalle, Frankfurt, Germany
May 1, Westfallenhalle, Dortmund, Germany
May 3, Palais de Sport, Paris, France
May 5, Eilenriedehalle, Hanover, Germany
May 6/7, Sporthalle, Cologne, Germany
May 9, Carl Diem Halle, Wurzburg, Germany
May 10, Sporthalle, Stuttgart, Germany
May 12/13, Stadthalle, Vienna, Austria
May 15, Waldbuehne, Berlin, Germany
May 16, Ernst Mercke Halle, Hamburg, Germany
May 18, Eissporthalle, Kassel, Germany
May 21, Olympiahalle, Munich, Germany
May 29, Elland Road Football Stadium, Leeds, UK
Jun 1 & 2, Ingliston Showground, Edinburgh, Scotland
Jun 5, Milton Keynes Bowl, Buckinghamshire, UK

North America

Jul 21, Forum, Montreal, Quebec
Jul 23, Boston Gardens, Boston, Massachussets
Jul 24, Spectrum, Philadelphia, Pennsylvania
Jul 25, Capitol Center, Washington DC
Jul 27/28, Madison Square Garden, New York
Jul 31, Richfield Coliseum, Cleveland, Ohio
Aug 2/3, Maple Leaf Gardens, Toronto, Ontario

Aug 5, Market Square Arena, Indianopolis, Indiana
Aug 6, Joe Louis Arena, Detroit, Michigan
Aug 7, Riverfront Coliseum, Cincinnati, Ohio
Aug 9, Brendon Burn Coliseum, Meadowlands, New Jersey
Aug 10, New Haven Coliseum, Connecticut
Aug 13/14, Poplar Creek, Chicago, Illinois
Aug 15, Civic Center Arena, St Paul, Minnesota
Aug 19, Civic Center, Biloxi, Mississippi
Aug 20, Summit, Houston, Texas
Aug 21, Reunion, Dallas, Texas
Aug 24, The Omni, Atlanta, Georgia
Aug 25, Mid South Coliseum, Memphis, Tennessee
Aug 27, City Myriad, Oklahoma
Aug 28, Kemper Arena, Kansas City, Missouri
Aug 30, McNichols Arena, Denver, Colorado
Sep 2, Portland Coliseum, Portland, Oregon
Sep 3, Seattle Coliseum, Seattle, Washington
Sep 4, PNE Coliseum, Vancouver, British Colombia
Sep 7, Oakland Coliseum, Oakland, California
Sep 10, ASU Arena, Temple, Texas
Sep 11/12, Irving Meadows, Irving, Texas
Sep 14/15, The Inglewood Forum, Los Angeles

Japan

Oct 19/20, Kyuden Auditorium, Fukuoka
Oct 24, Hankyu Nishinomiyakyujo, Osaka
Oct 26, Kokusai Tenjijo, Nagoya
Oct 29, Hokkaidoritso Sangyo Kyoshinakaijo, Sapporo
Nov 3, Seibu Lions Stadium, Tokyo

Typical Set List

Flash's Theme
Rock It
We Will Rock You
Action This Day
Play The Game
Now I'm Here
Dragon Attack
Now I'm Here (reprise)
Save Me
Calling All Girls
Back Chat
Get Down Make Love
Body Language
Under Pressure
Fat Bottomed Girls
Crazy Little Thing Called Love
Bohemian Rhapsody
Tie Your Mother Down
Another One Bites The Dust
We Will Rock You
We Are The Champions
God Save The Queen

QUEEN

///QUEEN///

Hot Space Tour '82

OFFICIAL PROGRAMME

The Hot Space tour of 1982 followed the release of Queen's disco-influenced studio album of the same name. The tour, which started in Gothenburg, Sweden in April 1982, saw many changes to the show. It was the first time, for instance, in which the band employed a keyboard player to perform in the background. For the European leg of the tour, they chose Morgan Fisher, best known as a member of Mott the Hoople in the 1970's. Having toured with Mott several years before, Queen already had a connection with him.

The tour began before the album was released. The delay was down to David Bowie, who'd completed backing vocals on one track – in addition to duetting with Freddie Mercury on the single 'Under Pressure'. Bowie felt his backing vocals weren't up to scratch and insisted the song be removed from the album with the result that, on the European leg of the tour, audiences were not familiar with heavily funked-up numbers such as 'Staying Power' and 'Body Language'. On hearing them live, many fans weren't impressed. At a concert in Frankfurt, jeers and heckling greeted Freddie Mercury when he announced the next song would be 'Staying Power'. 'If you don't want to listen to it, f**king go home!' he yelled back.

Neither were traditional fans enamoured with the tour support – punk-popsters, Bow Wow Wow. When the band were pelted with bottles while on stage, they responded by chucking them back and subsequently quit the tour.

'We liked them very much,' said Brian May. 'But there was this certain section of our audience who found them very modern. A small percentage of our audience, it's a sad comment, is perhaps a little narrow minded in that way.'

British band Air Race replaced Bow Wow Wow for the remaining dates.

Back in Britain at the end of May, there were more headaches when Queen were refused permission to perform at both the Ar-senal football ground in London and the Old Trafford Stadium in Manchester. A show at the Royal Albert Hall was cancelled when the venue's managers saw the size of the band's lighting rig and feared it would damage the listed building. Three shows were arranged at alternative venues – a showground in Edinburgh, a football stadium in Leeds and the Milton Keynes Bowl. This third date was filmed and broadcast on the UK's Channel Four the following year.

During this show, it was clear that Brian May had problems with his guitar. During 'We Will Rock You' and 'Dragon Attack', a couple of strings snapped and he had to switch to his back-up for entire second half of 'Dragon Attack', 'Now I'm Here' and almost all of 'Action This Day'. Further problems with the guitar became apparent during May's solo. The lead became disconnected and the guitar solo stopped for 20 seconds. A roadie had to help him get his instrument working again. Roger Taylor performed an impromptu 30-second drum solo while May got his guitar fixed. Freddie Mercury, meanwhile, camped it up a treat. He did, however, become a tad serious when introducing the funkadelic numbers from 'Hot Space'.

'Most of you know you've got some new sounds out last week. . . and for what it's worth we're gonna do some songs in the black funk category, whatever you call it. . . People get so excited about these things! It's only a bloody record.'

The MK crowd couldn't get enough of them, though. A journalist was filmed asking members of the audience why they'd come to see Queen. One punter answered for everyone. . .'Coz we love them – we love them all!'

Stage manager Rick O'Brien was also interviewed.

'What you want to do is create a 60 by 40 foot universe that never changes for the band,' he said. 'So, they just come up and play – whether it be in Argentina, Europe, or in the States – and on stage is the same wherever they go. The band shouldn't have anything

Freddie Mercury and Brian May of Queen perform on stage at The National Bowl on June 5th, 1982 in Milton Keynes, UK

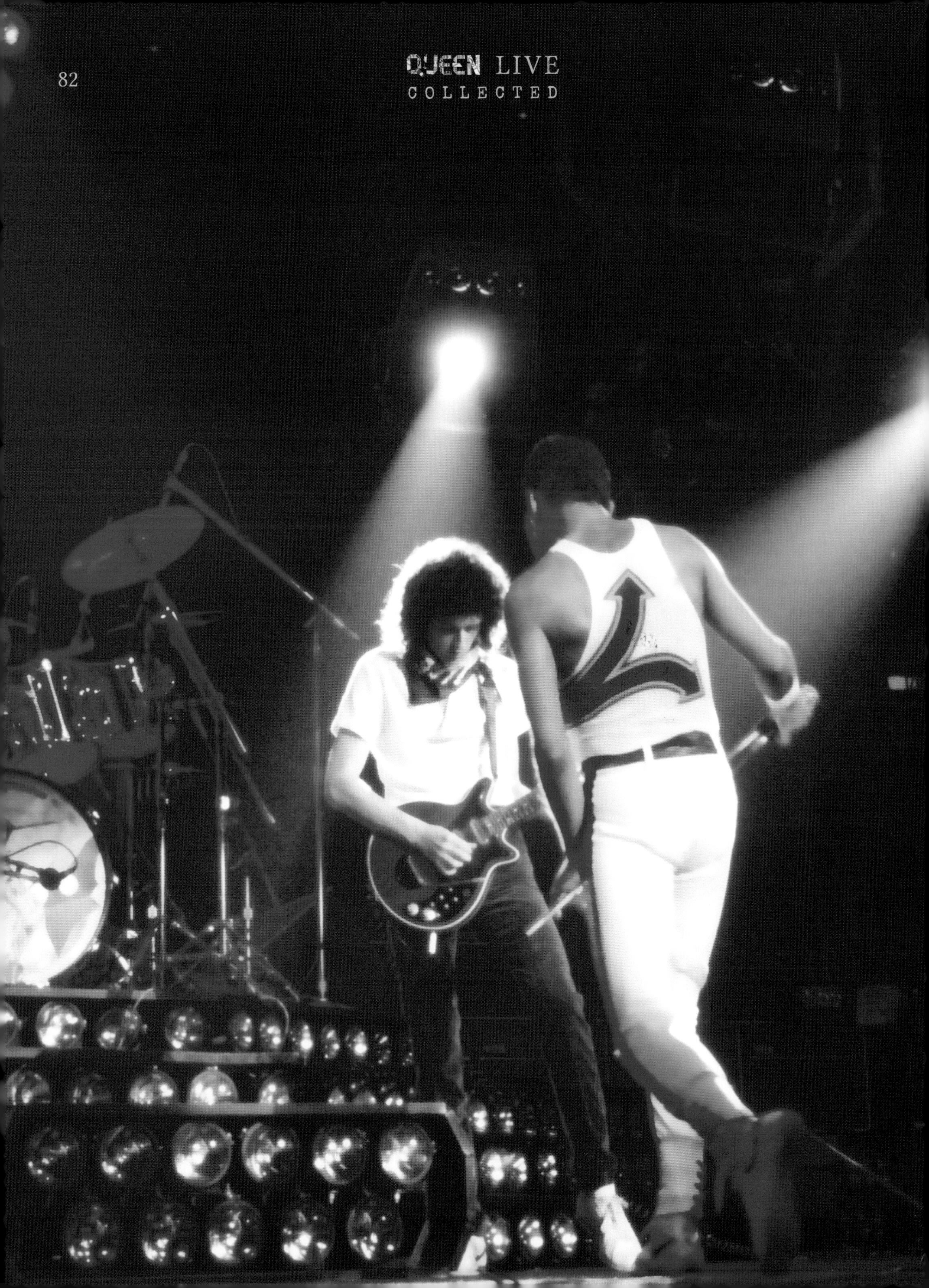

else to worry about apart from performing for the fans.

On July 18, Queen flew to Montreal for the seven-week North American leg of the 'Hot Space' tour, known, stateside, as the 'Rock n' America Tour'. The band had no inkling at the time but this would be their last outing across the pond. As in the UK, the sales for 'Hot Space', released in the US two months earlier, were disappointing with 22 being the highest chart position achieved. As the tour progressed, it slipped further and further down the charts. To rub salt into the wound, the album by support act Billy Squier was whizzing along in the opposite direction. But Queen were not resentful of his success.

'I remember Roger Taylor coming up to my dressing room after the Boston show to thank me for "Saving our ass on this tour",' said Squier.

Taylor, it seemed, had noticed that venues were not nearly so rammed as they had once been. This, plus the fact that the band were exhausted after years of the relentless recording/touring regime, and were also, quite simply, sick being with each other, caused tension. Queen had always argued in the studio but not usually on tour. Now they were. There were reports of raised voices in the dressing room after gigs, May uncharacteristically chucked his guitar into the wings when a string broke and refused to fly by private jet from venue to venue, feeling it was cutting him off from reality.

'For the first time, I didn't feel that this tour was making me very happy,' said May 'I've often felt that in the studio, but that's the first time I felt it on tour'.

Meanwhile, at one gig, Mercury complained that the front few rows of the audience were too ugly and said he wanted to hold a casting session before letting fans into the venues! The tour wrapped with two nights at the forum in LA but their latest US single 'Calling All Girls' had limped into the charts at Number 60 and not moved any higher.

Thankfully the Japanese leg of the tour was on the horizon. 'Hot Space' album had fared better here, making it to Number Six in the charts. As was customary, Queen were welcomed back like conquering heroes. The tour was short – two weeks, five cities, six shows – and for once the cavernous-like Budokan Hall was not amongst the venues. Part of the third show in Osaka was filmed for the band's own archive while at the final concert in Tokyo, at the massive Seibu Lions Stadium, the entire set was filmed and later issued in Japan on video – the very first commercially available footage of the band in concert.

Queen would not play live again for another year...

Onstage at Byrne Arena, East Rutherford, New Jersey, August 9, 1982

12|The Works Tour

'The criticisms are absolutely and definitely not justified'

Brian May defending Queen's decision to perform in South Africa

1984

Europe

Aug 24, Foret Nationale, Brussels, Belgium
Aug 28/29, Royal Dublin Society Showgrounds, Dublin, Ireland
Aug 21/September 1 & 2, NEC, Birmingham, UK
Sep 4/5/7/8, Wembley Arena, London, UK
Sep 12, Westfallenhalle, Dortmund, Germany
Sep 14/15, Sportspalace, Milan, Italy
Sep 16, Olympic Hall, Munich, Germany
Sep 18, Omnisports, Paris, France
Sep 20, Groenoordhalle, Leiden, Holland
Sep 21, Foret Nationale, Brussels, Belgium
Sep 22, Europhalle, Hanover, Germany
Sep 24, Deutschlandhalle, Berlin, Germany
Sep 26, Festhalle, Frankfurt, Germany
Sep 27, Schleyerhalle, Stuttgart, Germany
Sep 29/30, Stadthalle, Vienna, Austria

South Africa

Oct 5/10/13/14/18/19/20, Super Bowl, Sun City, Bophuthatswana (now Northern Transval)

1985

Brazil

Jan 12/19, Rock in Rio Festival, Rio De Janeiro

New Zealand

Apr 13, Mount Smart Stadium, Auckland

Australia

Apr 16/17/18/20, Sports and Entertainment Centre, Melbourne
Apr 25/26/28/29, Entertainments Centre, Sydney

Japan

May 7/9, Budukan Hall, Tokyo
May 10/11, Yogishi Swimming Pool Auditorium, Tokyo
May 13, Aichi Auditorium, Nagoya
May 15, Jo Hall, Osaka

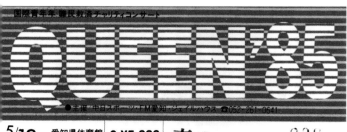

Typical Set List

'Machines
Tear It Up
Tie Your Mother Down
Under Pressure
Somebody To Love
Killer Queen
Seven Seas of Rhye
Keep Yourself Alive
Liar
It's A Hard Life
Dargon Attack
Now I'm Here
Is This The World We Created?
Love Of My Life
Stone Cold Crazy
Great King Rat
Brighton Rock
Another One Bites The Dust
Hammer To Fall
Crazy Little Thing Called Love
Bohemian Rhapsody
Radio Ga Ga
I Want To Break Free
Jailhouse Rock
We Will Rock You
We Are The Champions
God Save The Queen

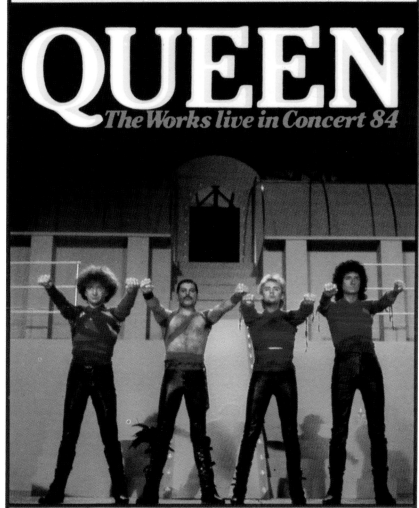

QUEEN

works!

WEMBLEY ARENA

HARVEY GOLDSMITH ENTERTAINMENTS
PRESENTS

QUEEN WORKS!

PLUS SUPPORT

Wednesday 5th September 1984
at 7.30 p.m.
(Doors open at 6.45 p.m.)

UPPER TIER NORTH
£8.00

TO BE RETAINED   See conditions on back

SEPTEMBER
5
1984

ENTER AT
NORTH DOOR
ENTRANCE

2

ROW
K

SEAT
17

HOLLAND CONCERTS PRESENTEERT
LIVE IN CONCERT
QUEEN
+ SUPPORT ACT
GROENOORDHAL - LEIDEN
DONDERDAGAVOND 20 SEPT. 1984 8 UUR
ENTREE f 27.50

Het is verboden om foto-apparatuur, film- en/of geluids-
opnameapparatuur, glas of blik mee de Hal te nemen
op straffe van inbeslagname. Officiële verkoop van
T-shirts e.d. slechts binnen de Hal. Koop niets buiten.

003496   QUEEN THE WORKS

WEMBLEY ARENA

HARVEY GOLDSMITH ENTERTAINMENTS
PRESENTS

QUEEN WORKS!

PLUS SUPPORT

Saturday 8th September 1984
at 7.30 p.m.
(Doors open at 6.45 p.m.)

WEST TERRACE
£9.00

TO BE RETAINED   See conditions on back

SEPTEMBER
8
1984

ENTER AT
NORTH DOOR
ENTRANCE

WEST
TERRACE

ROW
C

SEAT
34

DEUTSCHLANDHALLE

Autobus 4, 10, 65, 69, 92, 94   U-Bahn Kaiserdamm (Zubringer)   Deutschlandhalle

g, 24. Sept. 1984   Beginn siehe Rückseite

QUEEN
WORKS LIVE IN CONCERT '84
+ Vorprogramm

uppmann + Rau GmbH & Co. KG + concert concept Veranstaltungs-GmbH Berlin

nd · Programmänderungen vorbehalten · Haftungsansprüche sowie Kartenrück-
schlossen · Das Mitbringen von Tonbandgeräten, Filmkameras, Flaschen u. Dosen
lich nicht gestattet · Die Karte verliert beim Verlassen der Halle ihre Gültigkeit.

0211

Verbilligter Vorverkauf   Abendkasse   Kontrolle
DM 26,–   **DM 30,–**   Montag,
incl. 7% MwSt. + Vorverkaufszuschlag   incl. 7% MwSt.   24. 9. 1984

BIRMINGHAM INTERNATIONAL
ARENA
NATIONAL EXHIBITION CENTRE

HARVEY GOLDSMITH
PRESENTS

QUEEN WORKS

+ SUPPORT

DOORS OPEN 6:00 PM

£ 9.00

BLOCK
09

ROW
K

SEAT
41

FRIDAY
31ST AUG
1984
7:30PM

SOUTH
STAND

SOUTH

(including VAT)

TO BE RETAINED   (plans & conditions
see reverse)

Ref. 41999

WEMBLEY ARENA

HARVEY GOLDSMITH ENTERTAINMENTS
PRESENTS

QUEEN WORKS!

PLUS SUPPORT

Friday 7th September 1984
at 7.30 p.m.
(Doors open at 6.45 p.m.)

UPPER TIER SOUTH
£8.00

TO BE RETAINED   See conditions on back

SEPTEMBER
7
1984

ENTER AT
SOUTH DOOR
ENTRANCE

51

ROW
O

SEAT
7

FOREST - VORST NATIONA(A)L

Vrijdag 24 augustus 1984 - 20.30 u.
Vendredi 24 août 1984 - 20.30 h.

QUEEN

All glass containers, cans, firecrackers, fireworks, recorders and cameras excepting small
instamatic type cameras are strictly prohibited
in the hall and can be seized by artist
management and/or concert promotors.

550 Fr.   06927

Taksen en B.T.W. inbegr. - Taxes et T.V.A. compr.
TICKETS VOET - 9800 DEINZE

BIRMINGHAM INTERNATIONAL
ARENA
NATIONAL EXHIBITION CENTRE

HARVEY GOLDSMITH
PRESENTS

QUEEN WORKS

+ SUPPORT

DOORS OPEN 6:00 PM

£ 9.00

ARENA F

BLOCK
ARENA F

ROW
W

SEAT
17

SATURDAY
1ST SEP
1984
7:30PM

ARENA F

(Including VAT)

TO BE RETAINED   (plans & conditions
see reverse)

Ref. 41999

I n early February 1984, Queen reconvened to headline the annual San Remo song festival and two months later appeared at the Golden Rose festival in Switzerland where they mimed in front of 400 million TV viewers. They went back on the road proper in August 1984 on the 'Works' tour. In contrast to the start of the ill-fated 'Hot Space' tour, the Works album – featuring smash hits 'Radio Gaga', 'It's A Hard Life', and 'I Want to Break Free' – had been released several months earlier. By the time the tour began, to quote from the official programme, 'The album has gone either gold or platinum in over a dozen countries. The album's first single "Radio Ga Ga" was a massive worldwide hit, reaching number one in an incredible 19 countries. The follow-up, "I Want To Break Free", followed the tried and trusted Queen path, going gold more frequently than Sebastian Coe! And the Queen machine rolls on: a new single 'It's A Hard Life' looks set to follow its predecessors into the charts'.

The stage design for their first major tour in over a year was based on a scene from Fritz Lang's 1930 film, 'Metropolis', with two giant cog wheels that rotated at the rear of the stage, in front of a brightly lit cityscape, featuring several soaring sky scrapers. During 'Radio Ga Ga' strobe lights lit up the vast backdrop. There were also multiple levels – flights of stairs and catwalks for Freddie to strut along in addition to the main stage. This, however, came to be a challenge for him due to an earlier ligament injury in his knee.

Once again, learning from the 'Hot Space' tour, the set list was trimmed of funk numbers and instead harked back to the band's heavier canon of work. Opening in Brussels on August 24, before moving on to Dublin for two nights, they next played the Birmingham NEC for three, sell-out nights and the Birmingham Evening Mail couldn't sing their praises highly enough.

'NEC SHOW'S A REAL DAZZLER,' read the headline. 'Chart-topping group Queen began their three-night stand in Birmingham last night with one of the most spectacular shows the NEC Arena has ever seen. Back in Britain for the first time in two years, the four man group, who have scored numerous hits in the last decade, performed with enormous energy and enthusiasm for nearly two hours. . .While lead singer Freddie Mercury – clad for much of the show in just skin-tight red Spiderman trousers – strutted and pranced about the stage, the multi-coloured lights on the huge rig rose and fell and gigantic wheels spun against a mechanical landscape back drop. . . Queen, who have a reputation for producing excessive concerts, had promised their fans something special this time. None of them can have been disappointed. The only low point was when guitarist Brian May took a sustained – and by the end rather tedious – solo spot. Otherwise he, Mercury, drummer Roger Taylor and bass player John Deacon – with help from an extra musician and the special effects – held the audience's rapt attention. . . All the favourites from "Seven Seas of Rhye" through "Killer Queen" and "Under Pressure" were there and performed with staggering panache. So thrilled at the reception were the group that Mercury vowed they would keep playing concerts as long as their records sold.'

Four sell-out shows at Wembley Arena followed with Status Quo guitarist Rick Parfitt guesting on the 'Shake, Rattle and Roll' encore on one of the nights and Freddie responding to rumours that Queen were on the verge of splitting. 'They're all f**king untrue, right?' he roared at the crowd who roared their approval right back.' It was also at Wembley that he first donned the wig and false boobs he'd worn for the 'I Want To Break Free' video. Towards the end of the number, he sneakily sidled over to bassist John Deacon and shoved the falsies in his face!

On to continental Europe and during the Hanover gig, Mercury's injured leg gave way beneath him on one of the catwalks during 'Hammer to Fall'.

'I did a wrong move, fell down under the spotlights and they thought it was part of the show,' he was later to say. 'But I couldn't get up again.'

Carried to the piano, he was only then able to play 'Bohemian Rhapsody', 'We Will Rock You', and 'We Are the Champions'

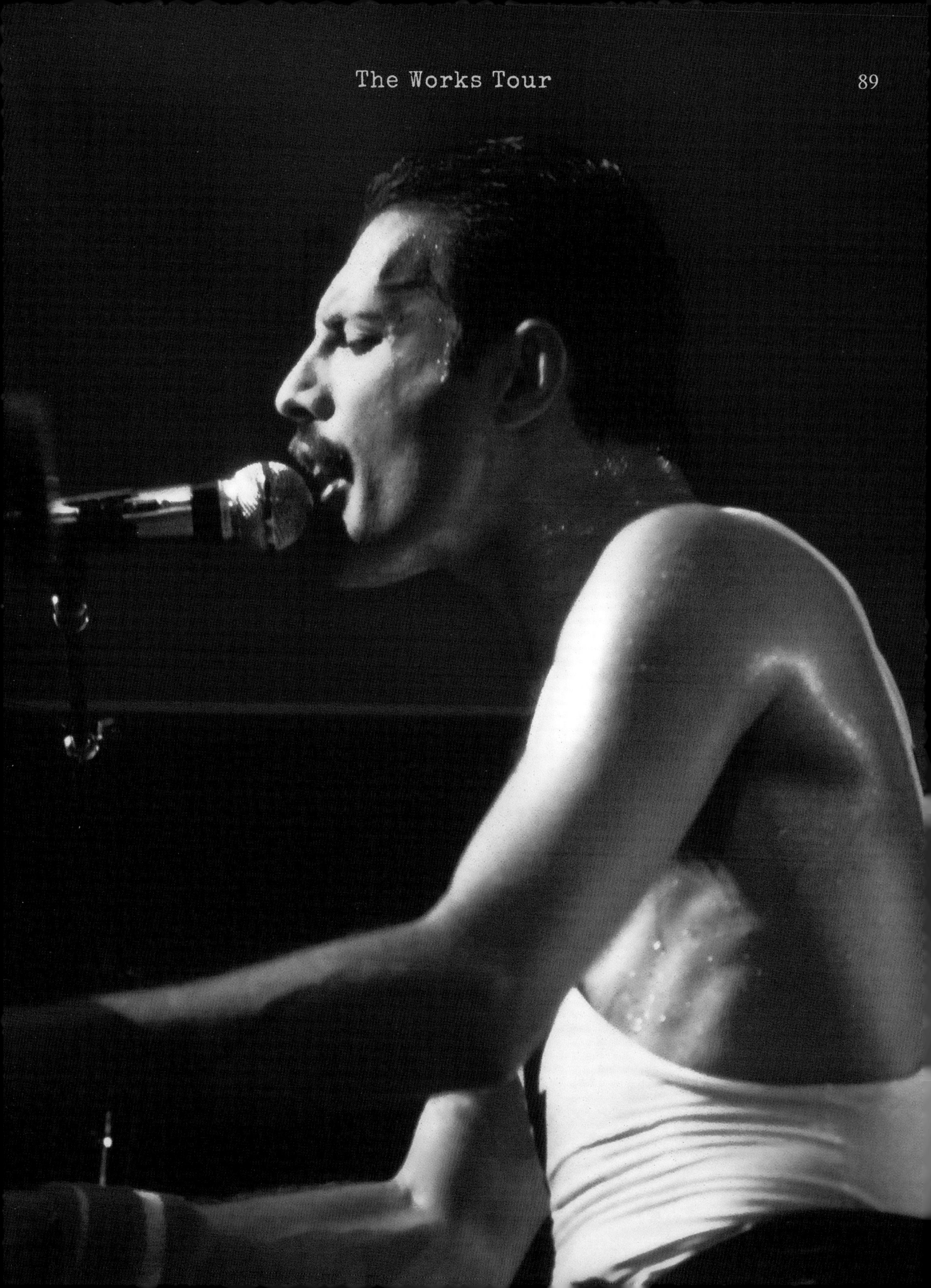

afterwards, shortening the concert somewhat. Due to Mercury's injury, May played the first bars of 'We Will Rock You' out of anxiety in order to give Mercury time to get to the hospital. He performed the remaining five European shows with a heavily bandaged leg.

On past tours after the European shows Queen had usually headed to North America. But that didn't happen on 'The Works'. Why not? Brian May seems to have had the answer.

'Freddie didn't want to go back to America and play smaller venues than we had before,' he was to later say. 'He was like, "Let's just wait and we'll go out and do stadiums in America as well". But it was one of those things that wasn't to be.'

Seven performances undertaken by Queen in Sun City, South Africa in October 1984 landed the band in extremely hot water. They were widely criticized for playing in a country where

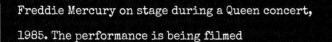
Freddie Mercury on stage during a Queen concert, 1985. The performance is being filmed

apartheid was then practised. The United Nations had asked entertainers to boycott the country plus Britain's Musicians' Union banned any of its members from performing there. But Queen decided to go regardless, defending their position by insisting they would play only to mixed audiences.

'The criticisms are absolutely and definitely not justified,' said Brian May in 1986. 'We're totally against apartheid and all it stands for but I feel that by going there, we did a lot of bridge building. We actually met musicians of both colours. They all welcomed us with open arms. The only criticism we got was from outside South Africa.'

The residency, originally supposed to be 12 dates, had been reduced to seven as Freddie was once again having problems with his voice. In fact, one concert was abandoned mid-show after his voice gave out altogether after 'Under Pressure'. However, he still managed to ruffle some feathers. His drag act during 'I Want To Break Free' was greeted by stones and cans lobbed from the audience. The song had become an unofficial anthem for black South Africans and was thus something that should not be taken lightly or made fun of. Mercury fortunately realised this in time and quickly abandoned the falsies and wig.

They followed South Africa with

another trip to South America. Their previous visit had ended badly but in early 1985, Queen returned. They had been booked to headline the opening and closing nights of the first seven-day festival Rock in Rio – the biggest music festival in the world. The Rio de Janeiro site, with a capacity of 350,000, took months to build and featured an enormous semi-circular stage with a massive fountain on either side.

Queen followed Iron Maiden onto the stage on the opening night of January 12 1985. They were two hours late – rumoured to be because Brian May was suffering from flu – and had to be helicoptered in at the last minute. All were dressed in white. Peter Hillman, a journalist from a British broadsheet newspaper covering the event, was stunned to witness the effect Freddie Mercury had on the massive crowd.

'He'd lift his hand and they'd sing along. He'd drop his hand and they'd fall silent. The effect was unbelievable. Like seeing a nuclear reactor split the atom.'

The Boston Globe were equally impressed, describing it as a 'mesmerising performance'.

When Freddie appeared with wig and falsies for 'I Want to Break Free', there was the same kind of response from the South American crowd as from the South African.

'A near riot erupted when the crowd of 350,000 began tossing

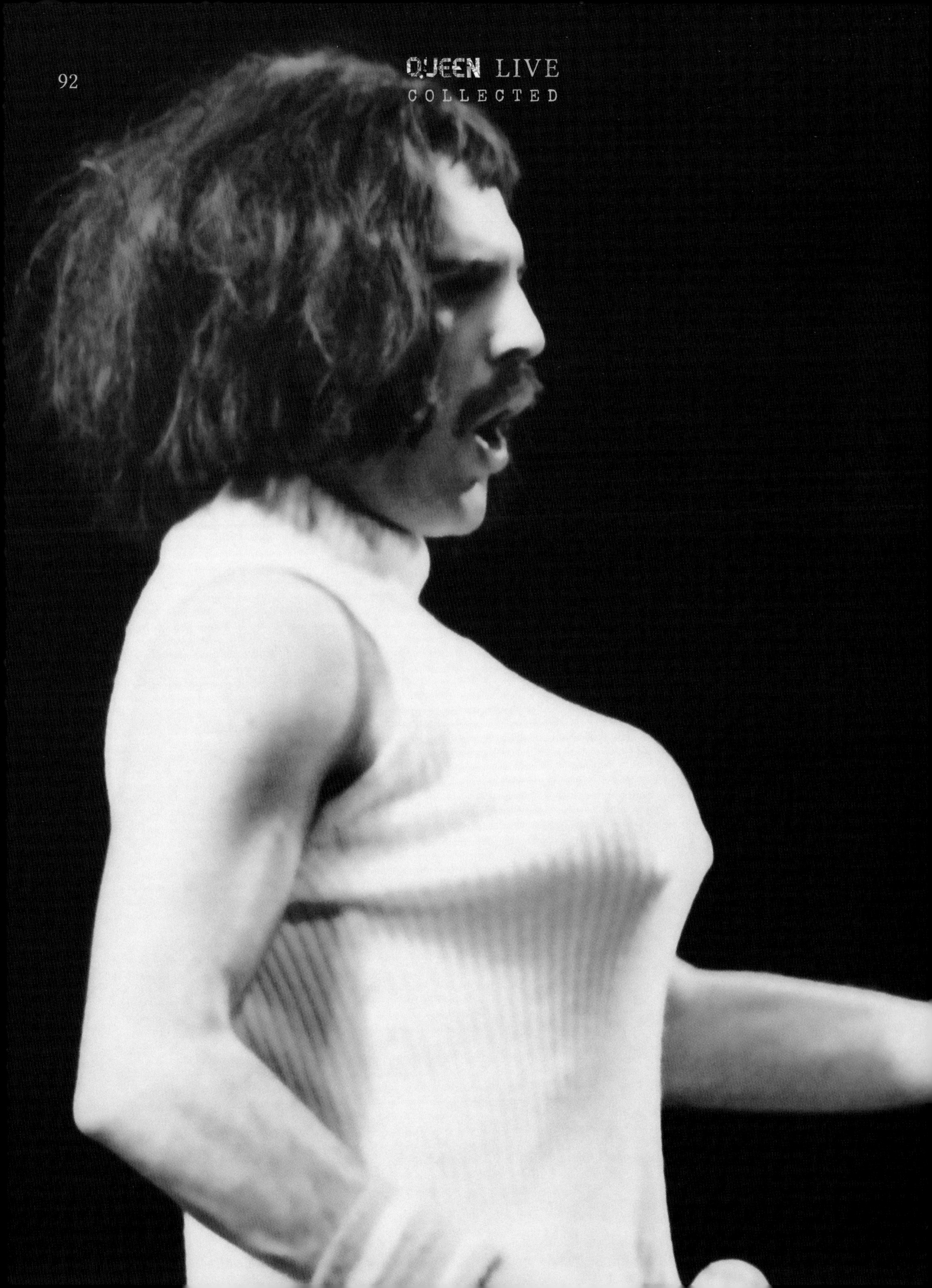

stones, cans and other weapons,' reported People magazine. Once again Mercury had misjudged the mood and quickly discarded the items, reappearing for 'We Will Rock You' and wearing a flag around his shoulders as a kind of cape. On one side was the British Union flag, on the other the Brazilian. The stadium erupted before Freddie threw the flag into the crowd. The show ended with a massive fireworks display.

The closing show on January 19 was filmed and released on video later in 1985.

'Rio was a wonderful audience,' Freddie went on to say. 'And I love their displays of emotion. They get over-excited sometimes but I can bring the whip down and show them who's in control. I don't know why they got so excited about me dressing as a woman – there are a lot of transvestites here.'

On April 5, Queen flew from London to New Zealand for their first ever gig there. It didn't start well. They were met by anti-apartheid demonstrators, at first, the airport and then their hotel. On the day of the concert, Freddie got drunk on vodka and port with Spandau Ballet vocalist Tony Hadley who also happened to be in town. By the time Freddie should have been getting ready to go on stage, he was totally out of it and had to be helped to get dressed. He managed to get through the set, adlibbing wildly. Hadley joined the band on stage for an encore of Jailhouse Rock but was still so drunk, he sang the words to 'Tutti Frutti' instead.

'Wrong song!' Hadley remembers. 'Freddie's going "Yeah – alright!" and Brian's going, "What the f**k is this?" The rest of them were just pissing themselves. Freddie and I didn't care – we were giving it loads. Simulating sex with Brian's guitar while he was playing it – the lot.'

From NZ, Queen travelled to Australia where they played four nights at the Sports and Entertainment Centre in Melbourne. Unfortunately, on the last night, the lighting rig stopped working halfway through the gig plus there were sound problems. A further four nights at Sydney's Entertainment Centre followed.

Queen travelled back to the UK briefly before jetting out to do six dates in Japan where, as always, they could do no wrong.

The Works Tour had been a success but it was hard to see where the band would go next. What else was there to achieve?

'When we first started, we were very future thinking,' said John Deacon addressing the subject. 'We wanted to do this or go there. We wanted our albums to be successful here, there and everywhere. But once we'd achieved that and been successful in so many countries in the world, it took away some of the incentive.'

Freddie Mercury was having similar thoughts.

'We were all forming a sort of a rut,' Mercury said at the time. 'I wanted to get out of this last 10 years of what we were doing. It was so routine. It was like, go to the studio, do an album, go out on the road, go round the world and flog it to death, and by the time you came back it was time to do another album. After a while it's like a painter… you know, you paint away, and then you stand back and look at it in perspective. That's exactly what we needed. We just needed to be away from each other, otherwise you just keep going in that routine and you don't even know if you're going down.'

Live Aid, the charity concert organised by Bob Geldof and Midge Ure to raise funds for relief of the ongoing Ethiopian famine, in July 1985 came at just the right time. . .

Wearing the costume used in the 'I Want To Break Free' video, Rock in Rio festival, Brazil, January 1985

13|Live Aid

'You bastards! You stole the show!'
Elton John to Queen after Live Aid Performance

July 13 1985   Wembley Stadium, London

Queen's 21-minute set at charity concert Live Aid has gone down in rock history as the best live performance of all time, yet initially they were unsure whether to take part.

'We definitely hesitated about doing Live Aid,' recalled Brian May – with Road Manager, Peter Hince, remembering that 'Freddie really needed to be talked into doing it.'

After finally accepting, Queen, aware of the calibre of the other musicians taking part – the likes of David Bowie, U2, The Who, Paul McCartney and Elton John – decided they needed to be prepared. Although they'd only come off tour six weeks earlier, they started rehearsing in earnest, booking out the 400-seat Shaw Theatre, near St Pancras train station in London, spending a week perfecting their five-song set and getting the timings precisely right so it would be as good as it possibly could be for the 72,000 fans at Wembley – and the estimated 1.9 billion people around the world watching on TV.

Bob Geldof had advised all the participants not to promote new hits but to do old favourites instead. Queen took him at his word – choosing arguably their six biggest hits which they altered and tweaked in order to fit the designated 20-minute time slot. When it came to choosing the time that they would take to the Wembley stage, they intelligently opted to go on at 6.41pm rather than later. This was close to prime time in the UK but also after the satellite feed from London had gone global, meaning that they would be the first band performing at Wembley who would also be seen in the US. Though the band did not like performing in daylight – and knew they

would have no sound-check to get the quality levels they preferred – they were well aware the concert gave them a chance to show the world what a great live band they were.

'It was our opportunity to show that it's the music first and foremost,' said May.

It was also for a very good cause.

'But I'm not doing it out of guilt,' said Freddie Mercury shortly before the event. 'Even if I didn't do it, the poverty would still be there. It's something that will always be there, to be honest, when you think about it. All we can do to help is wonderful things. I'm doing it out of pride, pride that I've been asked as well as that I can actually do something like that. And so basically I'm doing it out of feeling that one way all the hard work that I've actually done over the years has paid off, because they're actually asking me to do something to be

Typical Set List

Bohemian Rhapsody
Radio Ga Ga
Hammer To Fall
Crazy Little Thing Called Love
We Will Rock You
We Are The Champions

LIVE AID

WEMBLEY STADIUM
LONDON

JOHN F. KENNEDY STADIUM
PHILADELPHIA

JULY 13TH 1985

THIS PROGRAMME SAVES LIVES
PRICE £5

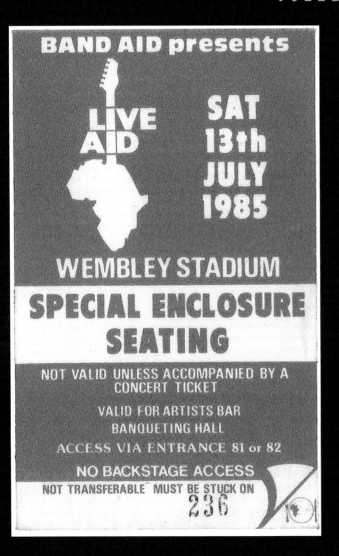

been examined by doctors.

'They said he was too ill to perform,' remembers a member of the Live Aid team. 'He wasn't well enough at all but he insisted.'

Incredibly, given his ill health, it was a truly charismatic Mercury, brimming with confidence, who jogged out on to a vast stage, followed by a nervous-looking May. Sporting his trademark moustache, Freddie wore white jeans, and a white tank top adorned with a banner saying 'Feed The World'. With a studded band around his right bicep, he began by sitting at the piano and playing a short, inspired version of 'Bohemian Rhapsody'. Queen were loud. Louder than any other band who had so far performed. This wasn't coincidental. Before going on, they'd sent their sound guy to check out the system and he craftily whacked up the volume.

'We were louder than anyone else at Live Aid,' Roger Taylor later admitted. 'You've got to overwhelm the crowd in a stadium'.

During 'Radio Ga Ga', Freddie strutted around the stage, using the microphone and stand as a prop, and getting the fired-up crowd to join in with the chorus. For the next few moments, he led the crowd in some spine-tingling vocal improvisation as they sang along to his 'ay-ohs'. His final, crystal-clear vocal was dubbed, 'the note heard around the world'.

The singalong fun was followed by a version of 'Hammer To Fall'. Mercury, who had strapped on an electric guitar, then addressed the crowd. 'This next song is only dedicated to beautiful people here tonight – which means all of you. Thank you for coming along, you are making this a great occasion,' he said, before launching into an energetic, exuberant performance of 'Crazy Little Thing Called Love'.

proud of. I'm actually in with all the biggies and I can do something worthwhile. To actually sing something that's an integral part of what's going on, you know, and the song 'We Are The Champions' seems to convey that anyway, without us thinking about it. That's what's magical, and I think that's going to probably bring tears to my eyes.'

On the day itself, Queen were immediately preceded at Wembley by the comedians Griff Rhys Jones and Mel Smith – who were dressed as policemen and joked about receiving a complaint about the noise 'from a woman in Belgium'. At around 6.44pm, they introduced 'the next combo' as 'Her Majesty... Queen'. No one was aware outside the inner sanctum that was the band but just an hour earlier, Freddie Mercury, who'd been suffering with a stubborn throat infection, had

After a short version of 'We Will Rock You', the swaying, completely enraptured crowd were treated to a finale of 'We Are The Champions'. Mercury was simply mesmerising – even to his fellow bandmates. 'I'd never seen anything like that in my life and it wasn't calculated, either... it was the greatest day of our lives. I'll never forget it,' said May.

Freddie Mercury on stage, Live Aid concert, Wembley Stadium. 13th July 1985

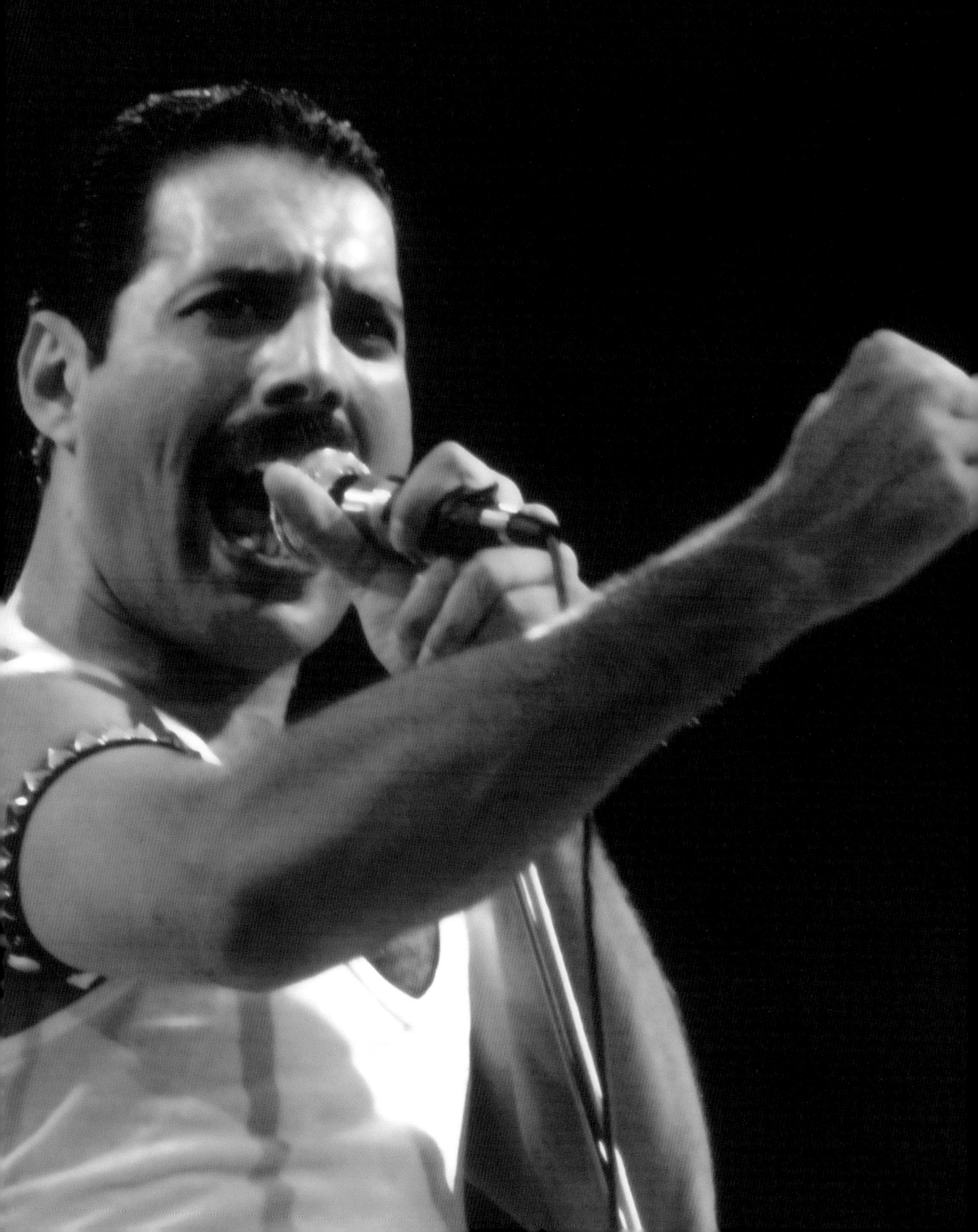

Queen at Live Aid on July 13, 1985 in London

It wasn't only Queen who realised that they had been sensational. 'You bastards, you stole the show,' said Elton John, having rushed to Mercury's trailer after the set.

Paul Gambaccini, who was part of the BBC broadcasting team at Live Aid, was struck by the reaction of other superstar musicians watching backstage.

'Credit must go to all of Queen for that phenomenal performance,' he remembered. 'When they went on, I was backstage interviewing artists for the TV broadcast. You could feel the frisson. All the artists stopped talking amongst themselves, stopped doing whatever they were doing and turned towards the stage. Everyone knew, as if was happening, that Queen were stealing the show. Freddie was doing his dance with the camera man in what was a blatant, sexually charged performance. They were rehearsed, they were ready, they were utter professionals. We thought," Oh my God, this is as good as a live rock performance gets". Queen were the best. When you think back to who else was on the bill, that's just incredible. Queen were over. They'd had their day. Yet here Queen were, reinventing themselves and going again before our very eyes. It still takes my breath away when I think about it. Freddie Mercury delivered the greatest front man performance anyone had ever seen.'

Bob Geldof agreed.

'Queen were absolutely the best band of the day,' the Live Aid organiser said. 'They played the best, had the best sound, used their time to the full. They understood the idea exactly, that it was a global jukebox. They just went and smashed one hit after another. It was the perfect stage for Freddie: the whole world.'

For Queen, it was a new beginning. After the Works tour, it had seemed like there was nowhere else to go and a split had seemed almost inevitable.

'We had been feeling jaded,' said Roger Taylor. 'Live Aid was a shot in the arm for us. A fantastic tonic. It was magnificent.'

It was time for a little more magic...

14|The Magic Tour

'I think we are probably the best live band in the world at the moment – and we are going to prove it. . . . Now we can't wait to hit the stage again.. It'll make Ben Hur look like The Muppets'

Roger Taylor on the eve of Classic Queen's final tour

1986

Europe

Jun 7, Rasunda Fotbolistadion, Stockholm, Sweden
Jun 11/12, Groenoordhalle, Leiden, Holland
Jun 14, Hippodrome De Vincennes, Paris, France
Jun 17, Foret Nationale, Brussels, Belgium
Jun 19, Groenoordhalle, Leiden, Holland
Jun 21, Maimarktgelande, Mannheim, Germany
Jun 26, Waldbuehe, Berlin, Germany
Jun 28/29, Olympiahalle, Munich, Germany
Jul 1/2 , Hallenstadion, Zurich, Switzerland
Jul 5, Dublin Castle, Dublin, Ireland
Jul 9, St James Park, Newcastle-upon-Tyne, UK
Jul 11/12, Wembley Stadium, London, UK
Jul 16, Maine Road, Manchester, UK
Jul 19, Muengersdorfer Stadium, Cologne, Germany
Jul 21/22, Stadthalle, Vienna, Austria
Jul 27, Nepstadion, Budapest, Hungary
Jul 30, Amphitheatre, Frejus, France
Aug 1, Monumental Plaza De Toros, Barcelona, Spain
Aug 3, Rayo Vallecano, Madrid, Spain
Aug 5, Estadio Municpal, Marbella, Spain
Aug 9, Knebworth Park, Stevenage, UK

Typical Set List

One Vision
Tie Your Mother Down
In the Lap of the Gods
Seven Seas of Rhye
Tear It Up
A Kind Of Magic
Under Pressure
Another One Bites The Dust
Who Wants To Live Forever?
I Want To Break Free
Brighton Rock
Now I'm Here
Love Of My Life
Is This The World We Created?
(You're So Square) Baby. . .
Hello Mary Lou
Tutti Frutti
Bohemian Rhapsody
Hammer To Fall
Crazy Little Thing Called Love
Radio Ga Ga
We Will Rock You
Friends Will be Friends
We Are The Champions
God Save The Queen

QUEEN WEDS 9th JULY 1986
NEWCASTLE

COMPLIMENTARY   AUDIT
                   092945

QUEEN WEDS 9th JULY 1986
NEWCASTLE

COMPLIMENTARY   SELLER COPY
                   092945

Harvey Goldsmith and

proudly presents

QUEEN

special guest stars

StatusQuo

Plus support

NEWCASTLE UNITED F.C
ST JAMES PARK
WEDNESDAY 9th JULY
1986

GATES OPEN 3 P.M.

Subject to Licence

COMPLIMENTARY   Do not bring **alcohol**, bottles, cans or tape recorders. No overnight camping. Ticket holders consent to the filming and sound recording of themselves as members of the audience.

COMPLIMENTARY
ST JAMES PARK NEWCASTLE
WEDS 9th JULY 1986

092945

HARVEY GOLDSMITH
PROUDLY
PRESENTS

QUEEN

Plus
Special Guests

KNEBWORTH PARK
STEVENAGE, HERTS
SATURDAY
9 AUGUST 1986

GATES OPEN 12 NOON
SHOW ENDS 10.30 p.m.

Subject to Licence

Advance tickets
£14.50 inc V.A.T.   Do not bring ALCOHOL,
On the Day   BOTTLES, CANS, VIDEO or
£16.00 inc V.A.T.   TAPE RECORDERS.

NO OVERNIGHT CAMPING
Ample Car Parking Available

Please keep the park tidy. Put your litter in
the bins provided or take it home. Thank you

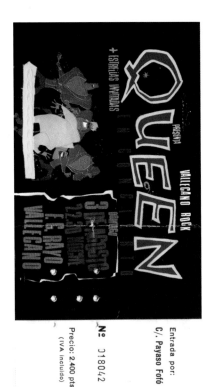

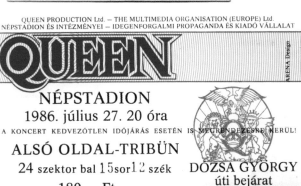

QUEEN

A Kind of Magic

EUROPEAN TOUR '1986

Inspired by their Live Aid triumph, Queen couldn't wait to go back on the road and also record new material. Things started to fall into place when they were asked to provide the music for the film, 'Highlander', starring Christopher Lambert and Sean Connery. Featuring tracks 'One Vision', 'A Kind Of Magic', 'Friends Will Be Friends' and 'Who Wants To Live Forever?', the album, Queen's 12th studio production, was released on June 2 1986. Prior to this, the band had spent the month of May in rehearsals and also planning their on-stage wardrobe. Costume designer Diana Mosley was gifted the task. 'You had to be gentle with Queen,' she recalled. 'You couldn't just rush and push things. Brian needed a little coaxing.' With regards to Freddie's look, h e and Mosley were inspired by Spanish opera and the military. He would be a rock soldier and wear military jackets with frogging – short and open to show a white T-shirt or chest hair. 'We had a little tussle with the colours,' said Mosley. 'He wanted yellow and I wanted red, but the compromise was the white because white always looks so good in the big stadium.' Since Diana was pushing him away from lycra, the trousers were looser. Th ey were white, but with a red stripe. As for the yellow jacket, even the frogging was yellow – Freddie's favourite colour.

Opening in Stockholm, Mercury appeared, the consummate showman he was, through a fog of dry ice. New songs were interspersed with old favourites with Queen wisely finishing up with their 'Live Aid' set. During this first show, sound engineers recorded that the audience vocal output was only a decibel less that the volume put out by the band's PA. After the gig, Mercury contacted Diana Mosley and requested she bring the newly commissioned fake ermine cloak and glittering crown to France in time for the Paris gig the following week. At the end of that show, during the dying bars of 'We Are The Champions', he sashayed regally onto the stage from the wings, wearing his regal garb, cradling his sawn-off mic like a septre and bestowing royal waves on the audience. This he would do for the remainder of the tour.

'He is the pivot of what it's all about,' commented Brian May. 'It's all channelled through Freddie.'

At the Mannheim gig, Queen were joined on stage for the 'Tutti Frutti' encore by the singer from their support band, 'Marillion' vocalist Fish.

'I kept thinking, "How the f∗∗k does it go?",' he remembered. 'Freddie had let me use his radio mic earlier with "Marillion" which was an unusual

Queen concert at Wembley stadium during the Magic tour on July 11, 1986 in London

thing to do, and he watched our show from the side of the stage. He welcomed me on for "Tutti Frutti" but then really put me in my place. Not in a nasty way but the sheer presence of the man on stage. . . He owned it. He was the big brother. I didn't stand a chance.'

The Magic Tour rolled on. . . It was proving to be extraordinary, smashing all UK attendance records of the time. The fans simply didn't want it to end. On June 11 and 12, Queen played Wembley Stadium - the scene of their 'Live Aid' triumph 11 months earlier.

'We're going to play on the biggest stage ever built at Wembley with the greatest light show ever seen. . .' Roger Taylor had promised. Along with the massive space which covered 6000 sq feet in total, were two huge Starvision screens. Almost as spectacular were the four huge inflatables - caricatures of Mercury, May, Taylor and Deacon - that were released into the air and floated towards the sky as Queen launched into 'A Kind of Magic'. The next morning one London resident was startled to find the deflated 'Freddie' nestling at the bottom of her garden!

A review of the second Wembley gig read, 'Freddie Mercury, the outrageous leader of Queen, reigned supreme at Wembley Stadium as he brought the house down amid plumes of smoke and brilliantly coloured lights. He whipped up the fans to fever pitch for the second night running and put himself among the all-time Rock n' Roll greats. Before last night's show, Freddie had feared his voice would fail. But once on stage, he pranced around in his king's crown and cloak, and sang encore after encore. Five electrical generators pumped 500,000 watts along miles of cable to operate the sound and lighting system - and the fans loved every minute of it.'

This gig was filmed was later broadcast on the UK's Channel Four where it was watched by 3.5 million viewers.

The band followed their UK Stadium dates with shows in Austria and Hungary, the latter of which was a communist country in 1986. Queen would be the first international rock group to play there. Playing to a capacity audience at Budapest's Nepstadion stadium, the book 'Queen - a Magic Tour' describes the band taking to the stage at the.

'Darkness fell, the noise of the crowd rose, the stage lights flashed even more brightly and the smoke billowed even more violently - and out of the mist, Queen came on stage. Freddie Mercury began to flash like the lights and chase the smoke around the stage. Roger Taylor crouched behind his drums pounding out the rhythm, seemingly intent of smashing them to oblivion; John Deacon's face was tight with concentration as he played his bass, and Brian May fought a musical duel with Freddie Mercury. "One Vision" was an apt title for the opening number.'

May and Mercury had also learned a couple of lines of the traditional Hungarian folk tune 'Tvaski Szel' which they inserted into the set. The audience erupted at this.

'Before, they hadn't known how to react,' said Brian May. 'But then they realised we were serious and the result was f**king deafening.'

The Budapest gig was filmed and made into an 85-minute documentary/concert film entitled 'Magic: Queen in Budapest', released the following year.

The Marbella show was to have been the last of the tour but such was the demand that promoter Harvey Goldsmith decided to book out the legendary venue that was Knebworth Park in Hertfordshire, England.

No one knew it at the time but this would be, as the classic Mercury, May, Taylor, Deacon line-up, Queen's last ever concert. Performing in front of a crowd estimated to number 200,000, Queen arrived by helicopter and pulled out all the stops. Garbed in his royal regalia, after the final encore Freddie surveyed his adoring subjects from the stage. His final words to the audience - any audience - were, 'Thank you, you beautiful people. Good night. Sweet dreams. We love you. . .'

Freddie Mercury dressed as a King during a performance with his group Queen at Wembley Stadium in London, 15th July 1986

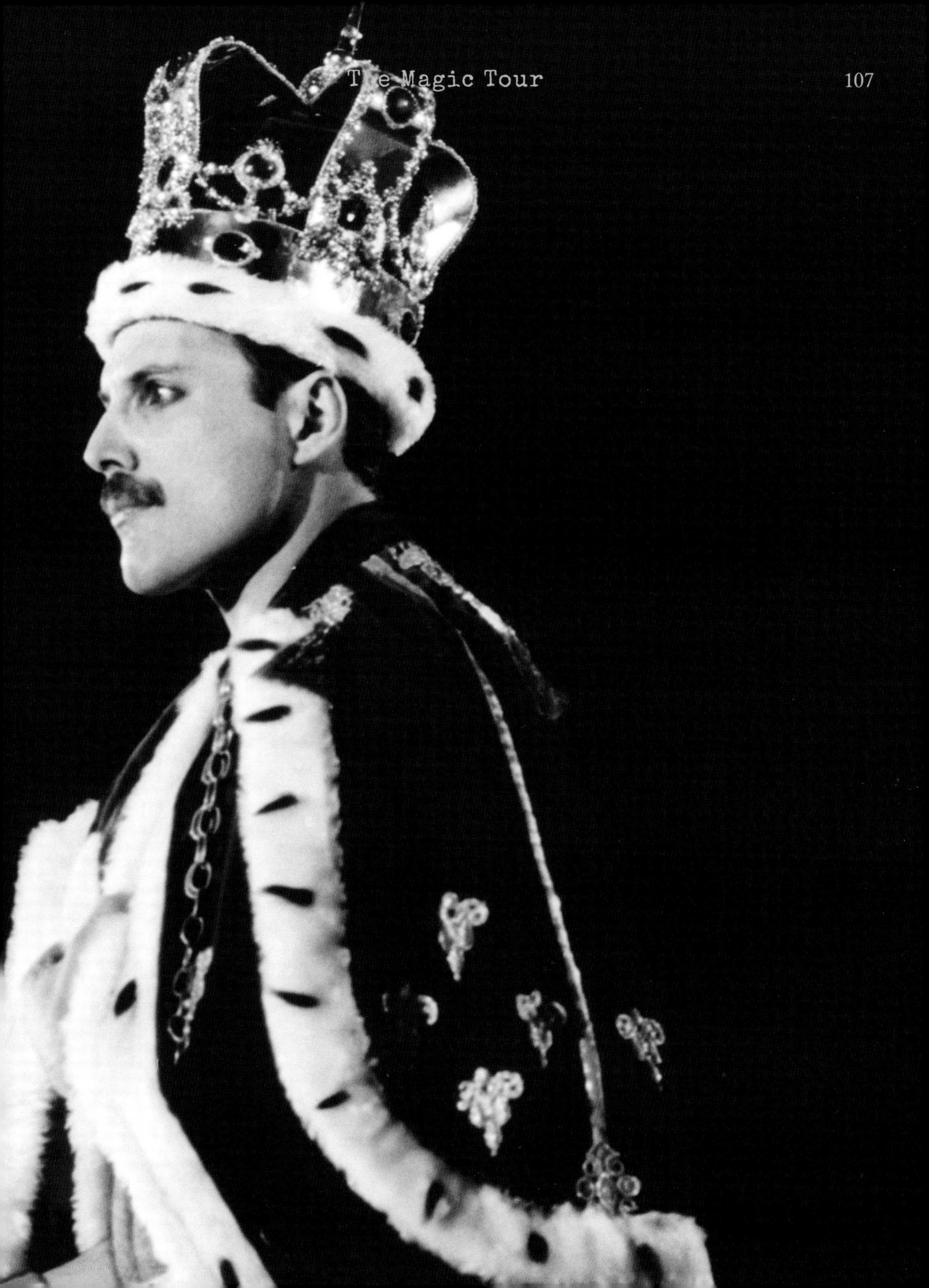

15 | The Freddie Mercury Tribute Concert

'We should give him an exit in the true style to which he's accustomed'

Brian May

Wembley Stadium – 20 April 1992

FIRST HALF

Metallica: 'Enter Sandman', 'Sad but True', 'Nothing Else Matters'

Extreme: Queen Medley – 'Mustapha', 'Bohemian Rhapsody', 'Keep Yourself Alive', 'Love of My Life', 'Fat Bottomed Girls', 'I Want To Break Free', 'Bicycle Race', 'Another One Bites The Dust', 'We Will Rock You', 'Stone Cold Crazy', 'Radio Ga Ga', 'More Than Words'

Def Leppard: 'Animal', 'Let's Get Rocked', 'Now I'm Here' with Brian May

Bob Geldof: 'Too Late God'

Spinal Tap: 'The Majesty of Rock'

U2: 'Until the End of the World' – played via satellite from California

Guns N'Roses: 'Paradise City', 'Only Women Bleed', 'Knockin' on Heaven's Door'.

Mango Groove: 'Special Star' – played via satellite from Johannesburg, South Africa

Elizabeth Taylor: AIDS Prevention Speech

Freddie Mercury: compilation of various interactions with the audience

SECOND HALF

Queen, Def Leppard's Joe Elliott and Guns and Roses' Slash: 'Tie Your Mother Down'

Queen, The Who's Roger Daltry and Black Sabbath's Tony Iommi: 'Heaven and Hell', 'Pinball Wizard', 'I Want It All'

Queen and Zucchero: 'Las Palabras de Amor'

Queen, Gary Cherone and Tony Iommi: 'Hammer to Fall'

Queen, James Hetfield and Tony Iommi: 'Stone Cold Crazy'

Queen and Led Zeppelin's Robert Plant: Innuendo', 'Thank You', 'Crazy Little Thing Called Love'

Brian May and Spike Edney: 'Too Much Love Will Kill You'

Queen and Paul Young: 'Radio Ga Ga'

Queen and Seal: 'Who Wants to Live Forever'

Queen and Lisa Stansfield: 'I Want to Break Free'

Queen, David Bowie and Annie Lennox: 'Under Pressure'

Queen, Ian Hunter, David Bowie, Mick Ronson and Def Leppard's Joe Elliott and Phil Collen: 'All the Young Dudes',

Queen, David Bowie and Mick Ronson: 'Heroes'

David Bowie: 'The Lord's Prayer'

Queen and George Michael: '39'

Queen, George Michael and Lisa Stansfield: 'These Are the Days of Our Lives'

Queen and George Michael: 'Somebody to Love'

Queen, Elton John and Axl Rose: 'Bohemian Rhapsody'

Queen, Elton John and Tony Iommi: 'The Show Must Go On'

Queen and Axl Rose: 'We Will Rock You'

Queen, Liza Minnelli and all the other artists: 'We Will Rock You'

Queen: 'God Save The Queen'

THE
FREDDIE MERCURY
TRIBUTE

CONCERT FOR AIDS AWARENESS

EASTER MONDAY APRIL 20th 1992

WEMBLEY STADIUM

THE
FREDDIE MERCURY
TRIBUTE

CONCERT FOR AIDS AWARENESS
ALL AREAS

WEMBLEY STADIUM   WEMBLEY STADIUM

00309849396072

THE
FREDDIE MERCURY
TRIBUTE
Concert for Aids Awareness

Concert
for Aids
Awareness

MONDAY
APRIL 20th
1992

MONDAY APRIL 20th 1992
GATES OPEN 4.00 PM   SHOW STARTS 6.00 PM

Profits to Aids Charities Worldwide

Enter by: TURNSTILE B

Subject to licence
No Bottles or Cans Permitted
Issued subject to conditions on reverse

Turnstile
No.
8786

8786
£25.00   £25.00

6   256 110392 152850A

On the evening of 24 November 1991, the day Freddie Mercury died from broncopheumonia brought on by AIDS, the three remaining Queen members gathered at Roger Taylor's Surrey mansion and decided to celebrate the life and legacy of the charismatic front man in a style he would have approved of. A tribute concert was decided upon which would also raise money for AIDS research and spread awareness about the disease. Three months later, on 12 February, Roger formerly announced the event - which would take place on 20 April 1992 at Wembley Stadium - at the BRIT Awards ceremony. He and Brian had collected an award on Queen's behalf for their Outstanding Contribution to Music. They dedicated it to Freddie. Within hours of going sale, all 72,000 tickets had been sold. John, Roger and Brian were involved in every stage of the planning, especially when it came to selecting which artists should perform. Every musician or band they approached accepted the invitation.

Guitarist Brian May admitted that he was extremely nervous before the beginning of the show, but not so much about the music; he rather feared he would forget to name someone. When the three remaining members of Queen walked onto the stage at 6pm on April 20 1992, Wembley erupted.

'We are here to celebrate the life and work and dreams of one Freddie Mercury,' announced Brian. 'We're gonna give him the biggest send off in history!'

And how! Metallica opened the show, followed by performances from acts including Def Leppard, Guns and Roses, Bob Geldof and spoof rockers Spinal Tap. U2 appeared by satellite from the US. Between bands, while roadies changed the stage for the following acts' performances, video clips were shown honouring Freddie Mercury. The first half closed with movie star Elizabeth Taylor giving an AIDS prevention speech, followed by a compilation of Freddie's most memorable interactions with audiences over the years.

The second half of the concert featured the three remaining Queen members along with guest singers and musicians. Not every performance was of 'Freddie standard'. The Who's Roger Daltrey couldn't quite reach the high tones on 'I Want It All', Paul Young's rendition of 'Radio Ga Ga' was a tad lack lustre, while Led Zeppelin's Robert Plant had problems remembering the lyrics to the epic song 'Innuendo' which Mercury had composed as a homage to Led Zeppelin.

'I tried to learn them while I was on holiday in Morocco, but I ended up with a huge lyric sheet taped to the stage,' Plant later said.

Other numbers have gone down in rock history. Arguably the most emotional was Brian May sitting at the piano, singing his own composition 'Too Much Love Will Kill You', which he dedicated to Freddie.

'My only excuse for playing it is, it's the best thing I have to offer,' he told the crowd.

Elton John and Axl Rose singing 'Bohemian Rhapsody' as a duet was another highlight. During the performance, the light show from the 1986 Magic Tour was used for the opera section. As a close friend of Freddie's, Elton John was one of the few people who'd visited him at the end of his life and had been invited to the funeral.

David Bowie sang 'Under Pressure' with Annie Lennox who replaced Freddie Mercury in the hit he had recorded with Bowie in 1981. Then, after singing 'We Could Be Heroes' with his old Ziggy Stardust band mate, Mick Ronson, Bowie went off-script by spontaneously going down on his knees and reciting the Lord's Prayer. This confused the audience - some even started to laugh. Bowie later admitted he wasn't quite sure what he was doing.

'I felt as if I were being transported by the situation,' he said. 'I was so scared as I was doing it.'

Robert Plant of Led Zeppelin performs with Brian May

George Michael offered the best performance of the evening. With his version of the Queen classic hit 'Somebody To Love' he captivated fans just as Freddie had during his peak.

'There was a particular point in the rendition that was pure Freddie,' Brian May was later to say.

For George Michael, it was a dream come true.

'It was probably the proudest moment of my career, because it was me living out a childhood fantasy: to sing one of Freddie's songs in front of 80,000 people,' he said.

'We Are The Champions' was held back for the finale, a perfect fit for Liza Minnelli, who put a bluesy spin on the iconic song and was supported by all those who had performed at the concert.

'Thanks Freddie,' she hollered. 'We just wanted to let you know, we'll be thinking of you.'

Queen's rendition of 'God Save The Queen' closed the show.

organization. However, backstage immediately after the show there was little of the usual post-performance euphoria.

'Immediately after the show was over, in private, it hit Brian very hard,' Tony Iommi was later to say. 'It hit them all and was so, so sad. John was just in bits. It was a case of, "Right, that's it, over, final". They had been very brave and it was highly emotional. There was this dreadful feeling of, "No more. It's finished".

'It would be wrong for us to go out with another singer, pretending to be Queen,' he said. 'I don't feel in my bones that we should keep Queen alive. I don't think it would be right for Freddie.'

While this would remain true for John Deacon, Brian May and Roger Taylor, history would tell a different story.

The Finale of the Freddie Mercury Tribute Concert for AIDS Awareness at Wembley Stadium on Easter Monday, April 20th 1992

16 | The Paul Rodgers Years 2004-2008

'We never thought we would tour again, Paul came along by chance and we seemed to have a chemistry. Paul is just such a great singer – he's not trying to be Freddie'

Roger Taylor

Return of the Champions Tour 2005-2006

Europe 2005

28 March, London, UK, Brixton Academy

30 March, Paris, France, Zenith

1 April, Madrid, Spain, Palacio de Deportes de la Comunidad

2 April, Barcelona, Spain, Palau Sant Jordi

4 April, Rome, Italy, Pala Lottomatica

5 April, Milan, Italy, Mediolanum Forum

7 April, Florence, Italy, Nelson Mandela Forum

8 April, Pesaro, Italy, BPA Palas

10 April, Basel, Switzerland, St Jakobshalle

13 April, Vienna, Austra, Wiener Stadthalle

14 April, Munich, Germany, Olympiahalle

16 April, Prague, Czech Republic, 02 Arena

17 April, Leipzig, Germany, Leipzig Arena

19 April, Frankfurt, Germany, Festhalle Frankfurt

20 April, Antwerp, Belgium, Sportpaleis

23 April, Budapest, Hungary, Budapest Sportarena

25 April, Dortmund, Germany, Westfalenhallen

26 April, Rotterdam, Netherlands, Rotterdam Ahoy

28 April, Hamburg, Germany, Colour Line Arena

30 April, Stockholm, Sweden, Globe Arena

3 May, Newcastle, UK, Metro Radio Arena

4 May, Manchester, UK, Manchester Evening News Arena

6 May, Birmingham, UK, National Exhibition Centre

7 May, Cardiff, UK, Cardiff International Arena

9 May, Sheffield, UK, Hallam FM Arena

11 May, London, UK, Wembley Pavilion

13 May, Belfast, Northern Ireland, Odyssey Arena

14 May, Dublin, Ireland, Point Theatre

2 July, Lisbon, Portugal, Estadio de Restelo

6 July, Cologne, Germany, Rhein Energie Stadio

10 July, London, UK, Hyde Park

Central/North America

8 October, Oranjestad, Aruba, Aruba Entertainment Centre

16 October, East Rutherford, USA, Meadowlands Arena

22 October, Los Angeles, USA, Hollywood Bowl

Asia

26 October, Saitama, Japan, Saitama Supe r Arena

27 October, Saitama, Japan, Saitama Super Arena

29 October, Yokohama, Japan, Yokohama Arena

30 October, Yokohama, Japan, Yokohama Arena

1 November, Nagoya, Japan, Nagoya Dome

3 November, Fukuoka, Japan, Fukuoka Yahoo! Dome

Typical Set List

Reaching Out
Tie Your Mother Down
I Want to Break Free
Fat Bottomed Girls
Crazy Little Thing Called Love
Say It's Not True
39
Love of My Life
Hammer to Fall
Feel Like Makin' Love
Let There Be Drums
Another One Bites the Dust
I'm in Love with My Car
Can't Get Enough
Last Horizon
These Are the Days of Our Lives
Radio Ga Ga
A Kind of Magic
I Want It All
Bohemian Rhapsody'
The Show Must Go On
All Right Now
We Will Rock You
We Are the Champions
God Save the Queen

2006

North America

3 March, Miami, USA, American Airlines Arena
4 March, Jacksonville, USA, Jacksonville Veterans Memorial Arena
7 March, Duluth, USA, the Arena at Gwinnett Centre
8 March, Washington DC, USA, Capital One Arena
10 March, Worcester, USA, DCU Centre
12 March, Uniondale, USA, Nassau Veterans Memorial Coliseum
14 March, Philadelphia, USA, The Spectrum
16 March, Toronto, Canada, Air Canada Centre
17 March, Buffalo, USA, Keybank Centre
20 March, Pittsburgh, USA, Mellon Arena
21 March, Cleveland, USA, Quicken Loans Arena
23 March, Rosemont, USA, Allstate Arena
24 March, Auburn Hills, USA, The Palace of Auburn Hills
26 March, Saint Paul, USA, Xcel Energy Centre
27 March, Milwaukee, USA, Bradley Centre
31 March, Glendale, USA, Gila River Arena
1 April, San Diego, USA, Cox Arena at Aztec Bowl
3 April, Anaheim, USA, Honda Centre
5 April, San Jose, USA, SAP Centre
7 April, Las Vegas, USA, MGM Grand Garden Arena
10 April, Seattle, USA, Key Arena
11 April, Portland, USA, Moda Centre
13 April, Vancouver, Canada, Pacific Coliseum

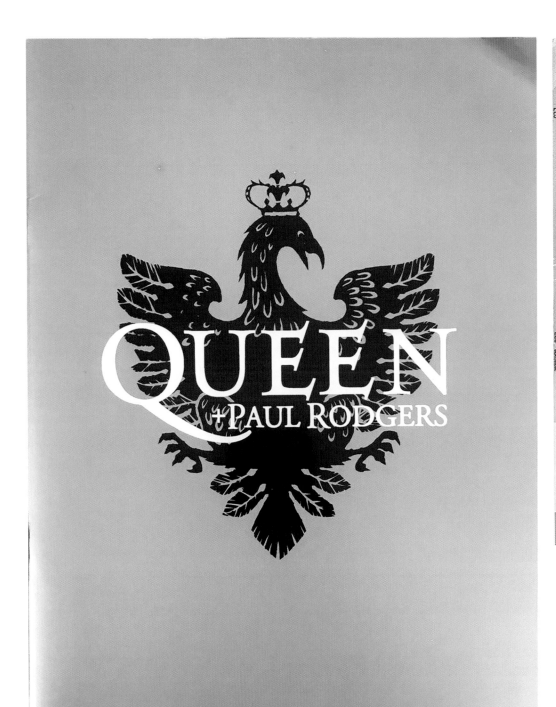

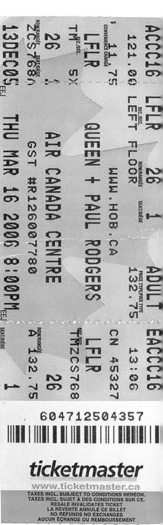

ACCC16   LFLR   26   1   ADULT   EACC16
121.00
LEFT FLOOR
11.75
www.hob.ca
QUEEN + PAUL RODGERS
132.75   13:06
AIR CANADA CENTRE   LFLR
GST #R126007780   CN 45327   TMZCS768   26
THU MAR 16 2006 8:00PM   A   132.75   1
13DEC05

604712504357

SHEFFIELD

MON 9th MAY 05 7:30 PM

Phil McIntyre Entertainment Presents

QUEEN + PAUL RODGERS

plus support

HALLAM FM ARENA
                    ROW   SEAT
BLOCK 102   E   5
DOORS OPEN 6.30PM   RED DOORS
£0.00   PLUS £0.00 BOOKING FEE
PROMOTER PRC0 9-MAY-05 (001.010)

M EN arena   SMG Europe   Manchester EveningNews arena

MA0405
FLOOR   STANDING   210   7
210 7   FLOOR
  9X   MA
AMX
49.50
ZMM434
25JAN5
08349   PHIL McINTYRE ENTS
                PRESENTS
22-14267   QUEEN+PAUL RODGERS
OGDEN/MR.   PLUS SUPPORT
  49.50   M.E.N. ARENA DOORS 6.00PM
SC 6.00   WED 04-MAY-2005 @ 7.30PM
  55.50

22-14267

M EN arena

105.4
centuryfm
www.1054centuryfm.com/myseat

Win Prizes online!
ticketmaster

Ticket Hotline: 0870 190 8000   www.men-arena.com

EUROPEAN TOUR 2005

The collaboration between Queen and vocalist Paul Rodgers of Free and Bad Company fame came about when Brian May played at an event marking the 50th anniversary of the Fender Stratocaster guitar in September 2004. Brian joined Paul on stage for a rendition of the classic Free track, 'All Right Now'.

'We'd just finished playing "All Right Now" and we both realised that it felt incredibly right,' said Brian. 'The chemistry was there, and there were sparks flying. Paul and me looked at each other and we went "Hmmm..." We both had the same thought in our minds. Then Paul's girlfriend said "All you need is a drummer, don't you?" And I said "Well, I might know a drummer..." That's kind of where it came from. I got the tape of our performance and sent it to Roger, and he said "Why didn't we think of this before?" Roger has always been the one who's been keen to get back out on tour. It was me who was holding things back because I didn't think things felt right. There was no one on the horizon who I thought could do the job of singing with us. And then suddenly we're looking at this man who can not only do the job, he can do a lot more besides – he brings something completely new to it and that's what turned me around. To be honest with you, if you'd spoken to me even nine months ago, I would've said "No, I'm never going out again – as far as Queen is concerned, that's it".'

The band would not be known as 'Queen' but 'Queen featuring Paul Rodgers' or 'Queen + Paul Rodgers'. Paul was adamant from the start that he was not a Mercury mark two.

'I am not trying to replace Freddie,' he said. 'I'm coming in to this as myself, playing some of their material and some of mine.'

In addition to May, Taylor and Rodgers, Queen + Paul Rodgers comprised of Queen's former touring keyboard player Spike Edney, rhythm guitarist Jamie Moses and bass guitarist Danny Miranda who had previously worked with Blue Oyster Cult. The first public performance was at a concert in South Africa in March 2005 in support of Nelson Mandela's AIDS awareness campaign. The tour officially started with a gig at the Brixton Academy in London. It was 19 years after the last Queen tour - the Magic Tour of 1986. An arena tour of Europe followed. The stage design for the tour was minimal, lacking a large backing screen and elaborate stage theatrics. However, a large 'B Stage' was constructed out from the main stage, projecting into the audience, which was used for acoustic performances. Opening with a rendition of Eminem's 'Reaching Out', the first segment of the concert consisted largely of Queen hits and some of Rodgers' songs.

To introduce 'Fat Bottomed Girls', Brian would play the introductory riff from the earlier Queen song 'White Man' while

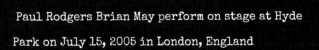

Paul Rodgers Brian May perform on stage at Hyde Park on July 15, 2005 in London, England

Rodgers often played a muted steel string guitar on 'Crazy Little Thing Called Love'. An acoustic section would follow, Taylor leaving the kit at times to sing 'Say It's Not True' on the B-Stage, while Brian would play Queen songs such as 'Love of My Life' and '39' acoustically. A unique version of 'Hammer to Fall' would be played, which featured a slower and mellower first verse sung by May and Rodgers. Taylor would often play an intricate cover of Sandy Nelson drum instrumental 'Let There Be Drums', followed by a performance of 'I'm in Love with My Car', with Taylor taking lead vocals and the drum parts. He would leave the kit to sing 'These Are the Days of Our Lives', with a screen playing nostalgic footage, including shots of the band on their early tours in Japan. 'Radio Ga Ga' would follow, with Taylor singing the first and second verses, and Rodgers the rest of the song. During 'Bohemian Rhapsody', Freddie's vocal and piano parts, along with video footage from Queen's 1986 show at Wembley Stadium, would be played, while the rest of the band would

Brian May performs at Hyde Park on July 15, 2005, London, England

play live music with Rodgers singing the heavier parts. The song would end with footage of Freddie taking a bow to the crowd, and the band would leave the stage. 'The Show Must Go On', 'All Right Now', 'We Will Rock You' and 'We Are the Champions' were performed as encores.

Reviews were favourable for this Queen/Bad Company combo.

'The show is a major success,' proclaimed Classic Rock magazine. 'And, given the public's continuing hunger for all things Queen, it will be fascinating to see how they choose to expand this Q+PR experiment further.'

Queen + Paul Rodgers followed the European tour with a series of performances in Japan and the US. Slash, lead guitarist with Guns N Roses joined the band for 'Can't Get Enough' during their show at the Hollywood Bowl. Queen received the inaugural VH1 Rock Honours in Las Vegas in May 2006. The Foo Fighters performed 'Tie Your Mother Down' to open the ceremony before being joined on stage by May, Taylor and Rodgers, who played a selection of Queen hits.

Such was the success of the tour, on 15 August 2006 Brian May confirmed that Queen + Paul Rodgers would begin producing their first studio album that October. The album, titled 'The Cosmos Rocks' was released in the Europe on 15 September 2008 and in the United States on 28 October 2008. In autumn 2008, Queen and Paul Rodgers set out on the Rock the Cosmos Tour to promote it.

Rock the Cosmos Tour 2008

Europe

12 September, Kharkiv, Ukraine, Freedom Square

15/16 September, Moscow, Russia, Olimpiyskiy

19 September, Riga, Latvia, Arena Riga

21 September, Berlin, Germany, Berlin Velodrome

23 September, Antwerp, Belgium, Sportpaleis

24 September, Paris, France, Palais Omnisports de Paris-Bercy

26 September, Rome, Italy, Palalottomatica

28 September, Milan, Italy, Datchforum

29 September, Zurich, Switzerland, Hallenstadion

1 October, Munich, Germany, Olympiahalle

2 October, Mannheim, Germany, SAP Arena

4 October, Hanover, Germany, TUI Arena

5 October, Hamburg, Germany, Colour Line Arena

7 October, Rotterdam, Netherlands, Rotterdam Ahoy

8 October, Esch-sur-Alzette, Luxembourg, Rockhal

10 October, Nottingham, UK, Nottingham Arena

11 October, Glasgow, UK, Scottish Exhibition and Conference Centre

13 October, London, UK, The O2 Arena

14 October, Cardiff, UK, Cardiff International Arena

16 October, Birmingham, UK, National Indoor Arena

18 October, Liverpool, UK, Echo Arena

19 October, Sheffield, UK, Sheffield Arena

22 October, Barcelona, Spain, Palau Sant Jordi

24 October, Murcia, Spain, Estadio de La Condomina

25 October, Madrid, Spain, Palacio de Deportes de la Comunidad

28 October, Budapest, Hungary, Papp Laszlo Budapest Sportarena

29 October, Belgrade, Serbia, Belgrade Arena

31 October, Prague, Czech Republic, O2 Arena

1 November, Vienna, Austria, Wiener Stadthalle

4 November, Newcastle, UK, Metro Radio Arena

5 November, Manchester, UK, Manchester Evening News Arena

7 November, London, UK, The O2 Arena

8 November, London, UK, Wembley Arena

Middle East

14 November, Dubai, United Arab Emirates, Dubai Festival City

South America

19 November, Santiago, Chile, Estadio San Carlos de Apoquindo

21 November, Buenos Aires, Argentina, Jose Amalfitani Stadium

26/27 November, Sao Paulo, Brazil, Via Funchal

29 November, Rio de Janeiro, HSBC Arena

Typical Set List

Hammer to Fall
Tie Your Mother Down
Fat Bottomed Girls
I Want It All
Surf's Up...School's Out
I Want to Break Free
C-lebrity
Seagull
Love of My Life
39
I'm in Love with My Car
A Kind of Magic
Say It's Not True
Bad Company
We Believe
Bijou
Lost Horizon
Crazy Little Thing Called Love
Radio Ga Ga
The Show Must Go On
Bohemian Rhapsody
Cosmos Rockin
All Right Now
We Will Rock You
We Are the Champions
God Save the Queen'.

Paul Rodgers of Queen performs at the O2 Arena,

October 13, 2008, London, England

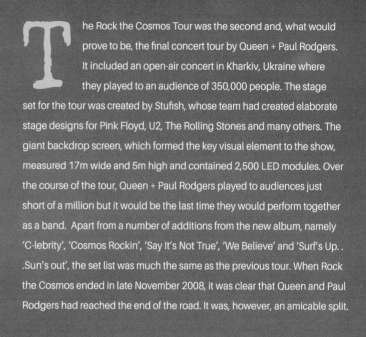

The Rock the Cosmos Tour was the second and, what would prove to be, the final concert tour by Queen + Paul Rodgers. It included an open-air concert in Kharkiv, Ukraine where they played to an audience of 350,000 people. The stage set for the tour was created by Stufish, whose team had created elaborate stage designs for Pink Floyd, U2, The Rolling Stones and many others. The giant backdrop screen, which formed the key visual element to the show, measured 17m wide and 5m high and contained 2,500 LED modules. Over the course of the tour, Queen + Paul Rodgers played to audiences just short of a million but it would be the last time they would perform together as a band. Apart from a number of additions from the new album, namely 'C-lebrity', 'Cosmos Rockin', 'Say It's Not True', 'We Believe' and 'Surf's Up. . .Sun's out', the set list was much the same as the previous tour. When Rock the Cosmos ended in late November 2008, it was clear that Queen and Paul Rodgers had reached the end of the road. It was, however, an amicable split.

'I just think that Paul's more blues and soul,' Brian May explained. 'He's one of our favourite singers ever, but when it boils down to it, he wasn't the perfect front man for us.'

Roger Taylor agreed.

'Paul was his own man,' he said. 'He belonged in the blues-soul field, at which there were none better. He wasn't the best front man for us. Our stuff is a little too eclectic probably, so I think that's why that came to an end.'

Rodgers, too, was philosophical.

'It was a wild ride,' he said. 'It lasted a lot longer than I had planned. Originally, we were just going to do a tour of Europe, just for fun, because it was so enjoyable to play together. And that turned into four years, during which we toured the world twice, and I went to all kinds of places I had never been before. We recorded a few live DVDs and finished off with a studio album of original material. Now it is time for me to get back, full on, to do my own thing — my own music.'

Rodgers re-joined his primary band Bad Company but neither was this the end of life on the road for May and Taylor. A certain Adam Lambert was waiting in the wings. . .

17 | Queen + Adam Lambert

'Adam looks fantastic, he's funny, sings beautifully and is a great showman. He's one of the best singers in the world and is the only person that really fills the boots of Freddie Mercury'

Roger Taylor

2012 Typical Set List

Intro: Flash's Theme (tape)
The Hero
Seven Seas of Rhye
Keep Yourself Alive
We Will Rock You
Fat Bottomed Girls
Don't Stop Me Now
Under Pressure
I Want It All
Who Wants to Live Forever
A Kind of Magic
These Are The Days of our Lives
Love of My Life
39
Dragon Attack
Last Horizon
I Want to Break Free
Another One Bites the Dust
Radio Ga Ga
Somebody to Love
Crazy Little Thing Called Love
The Show Must Go On
Bohemian Rhapsody

Encores

Tie Your Mother Down
We Will Rock You
We Are The Champions
God Save The Queen

2012 Tour Dates

30 June, Maidan Nezalezhnosti, Kiev, Ukraine
3 July, Olimpiyskiy, Moscow, Russia
7 July, Stadion Miejski, Wroclaw, Poland
11/12/14 July, Hammersmith Apollo, UK

2014–2015 Tour Dates

2014

North America
19 June, United Center, Chicago, USA
21 June, Bell MTS Place, Winnipeg, Canda
23 June, Credit Union Centre, Saskatoon, Canada
24 June, Rexall Place, Edmonton, Canada
26 June, Scotiabank Saddledome, Calgary, Canada
28 June, Rogers Arena, Vancouver, Canada
1 July, SAP Center, San Jose, USA
3 July, The Forum, Inglewood, USA
5-6 July, The Joint, Las Vegas, USA
9 July, Toyota Center, Houston, USA
10 July, American Airlines Center, Dallas, USA
12 July, The Palace of Auburn Hills, Auburn Hills, USA
13 July, Air Canada Centre, Toronto, Canada
14 July, Bell Centre, Montreal, Canada
16 July, Wells Fargo Center, Philadelphia, USA

17 July, Madison Square Garden, New York City, USA

19 July, Mohegan Sun Arena, Uncasville, USA

20 July, Merriweather Post Pavilion, USA

22 July, TD Garden, Boston, USA

23 July, Meadowlands Arena, East Rutherford, USA

25 July, Mohegan Sun Arena, Uncansville, USA

26 July, Boardwalk Hall, Atlantic City, USA

28 July, Air Canada Centre, Toronto, Canada

Asia

14 August, Jamsil Sports Complex, Seoul, South Korea

16 August, Maishima Sports Island, Osaka, Japan

17 August, Chiba Marine Stadium, Chiba, Japan

Oceania

22 August, Perth Arena, Perth, Australia

Sheffield
Ticketing Network

Fri 27 Feb - 2015 - 8:00PM
MOTORPOINT ARENA SHEFFIELD
Phil McIntyre Entertainments
Proudly Presents
Queen + Adam Lambert
Live 2015

BLOCK 203   Row
             L   4
Doors Open:7:00PM   Entrance:RED DOORS
£69.00   PLUS £6.90 BOOKING FEE
Tickets   ORDER #3435334
                     27-02-2015

26-27 August, Allphones Arena, Sydney, Australia

29-30 August, Rod Laver Arena, Melbourne, Australia

1 September, Brisbane Entertainment Centre, Brisbane,

Australia

3-4 September, Vector Arena, Auckland, New Zealand

Europe

31 December, Central Hall Westminster, London, England

2015

Europe (cont)

13 January, Metro Radio Arena, Newcastle, England

14 January, The SSE Hydro, Glasgow, Scotland

17-18 January, The O2 Arena, London, England

20 January, First Direct Arena, Leeds, England

21 January, Manchester Arena, Manchester, England

23 January, Barclaycard Arena, Birmingham, England

24 January, Capital FM Arena, Nottingham, England

26 January, Zenith de Paris, Paris, France

29 January, Lanxess Arena, Cologne, Germany

30 January, Ziggo Dome, Amsterdam, Netherlands

1 February, Wiener Stadthalle, Vienna, Austria

2 February, Olympiahalle, Munich, Germany

4 February, O2 World Berlin, Berlin, Germany

5 February, O2 World Hamburg, Hamburg, Berlin, Germany

7 February, Festhalle Frankfurt, Frankfurt, Germany

10 February, Mediolanum Forum, Milan, Italy

13 February, Hanns-Martin-Schleyer-Halle, Stuttgart, Germany

15 February, Jyske Bank Boxen, Herning, Denmark

2014-15 Typical Set List

Procession
Now I'm Here
Stone Cold Crazy
Another One Bites the Dust
Fat Bottomed Girls
In the Lap of the Gods - Revisited
Seven Seas of Rhye
Killer Queen
Somebody to Love
I Want It All
Love of My Life
39
These Are the Days of Our Lives
Under Pressure
Love Kills
Who Wants to Live Forever
Lost Horizon
Tie Your Mother Down
Crazy Little Thing Called Love
The Show Must Go On
Bohemian Rhapsody

Encore:

We Will Rock You
We Are the Champions
God Save The Queen

17 February, O2 Arena, Prague, Czech Republic

19 February, Hallenstadion, Zurich, Switzerland

21 February, Tauron Arena, Krakow, Poland

24 February, Wembley Arena, London, England

26 February, Echo Arena, Liverpool, England

27 February, Motorpoint Arena, Sheffield, England

South America

16 September, Ginasio de Ibirapuera, Sao Paulo, Brazil

18 September, New City of Rock, Rio de Janiero, Brazil

21 September, Gigantinho, Porto Alegre, Brazil

25 September, Estadio G.E.B.A, Buenos Aires, Argentina

27 September, Orfeo Superdomo, Cordoba, Argentina

30 September, Estadio Nacional Julio Martinez Pradanos, Santiago, Chile

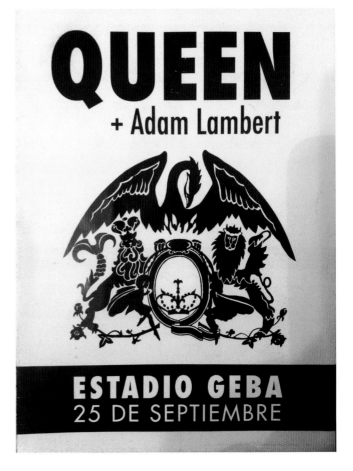

2016 Typical Set List

One Vision
Hammer to Fall
Seven Seas Of Rhye
Stone Cold Crazy
Another One Bites The Dust
Fat Bottomed Girls
Play The Game
Killer Queen
Don't Stop Me Now
Somebody to Love
Love of My Lif
A Kind Of Magic
Under Pressure
Crazy Little Thing Called Love
I Want To Break Free
I Want It All
Who Wants To Live Forever
Tie Your Mother Down
Bohemian Rhapsody
Radio Ga Ga

Encores:
We Will Rock You
We Are the Champions
God Save The Queen

The Summer Festival Tour 2016

Europe

20 May, Bela Vista Park, Lisbon, Portugal

22 May, Palau Sant Jordi, Barcelona, Spain

25 May, Linzer Stadion, Linz, Austria

27 May, RheinEnergieStadion, Cologne, Germany

29 May, Jelling Festival Grounds, Jelling, Denmark

3 June, Kaisaniemi Park, Helsinki, Finland

5 June, Tallinn Song Festival Grounds, Tallinn, Estonia

9 June, Solvesborg Norje, Solvesborg, Sweden

10 June, Isle of Wight Festival, Isle of Wight, England

15 June, Palais 12, Brussels, Belgium

17 June, Autobahnkreisal, Zurich, Switzerland

19 June, Stadion Sportowy MOSIR, Oswiecim, Poland

21 June, Piata Constitutiei, Bucharest, Romania

23 June, Georgi Asparuhov Stadium, Sofia, Bulgaria

25 June, Villa Contarini, Padua, Italy

Middle East

12 September, Yarkon Park, Tel Aviv, Israel

Asia

17 September, F1 Marina Bay Street, Singapore
19 September, Nangang Exhibition Hall, Taipei, Taiwan
21-22 September, Nippon Budokan, Tokyo, Japan
26 September, Mercedes Benz Arena, Shanghai, China
28 September, AsiaWorld-Arena, Hong Kong
30 September, Impact Arena, Bangkok, Thailand

2017-18 Typical Set List

We Will Rock You (teaser)
Hammer to Fall
Stone Cold Crazy
Another One Bites the Dust
Fat Bottomed Girls
Killer Queen
Two Fux
Don't Stop Me Now
Bicycle Race
I'm in Love With My Car
Get Down
Make Love
I Want It All
Love of My Life
Somebody to Love
Crazy Little Thing Called Love
Drum Battle
Under Pressure
I Want to Break Free
Who Wants to Live Forever
Guitar Solo
Radio Ga Ga
Bohemian Rhapsody

Encores:
We Will Rock You
We Are the Champions
God Save The Queen

2017-18 Tour
2017

North America

23 June, Gila River Arena, Phoenix, USA
24 June, T-Mobile Arena, Las Vegas, USA
26 June, Hollywood Bowl, Los Angeles, USA
29 June, SAP Center, San Jose, USA
1 July, Key Arena, Seattle, USA
2 July, Rogers Arena, Vancouver, Canada
4 July, Rogers Place, Edmonton, Canada
6 July, Pepsi Center Arena, Denver, USA
8 July, Century Link Center, Omaha, USA
9 July, Sprint Center, Kansas City, USA
13 July, United Center, Chicago, USA
14 July, Xcel Energy Center, St Paul, USA
17 July, Bell Centre, Montreal, Canada
18 July, Air Canada Centre, Toronto, Canada
20 July, The Palace of Auburn Hills, Detroit, USA
21 July, Quicken Loans Arena, Cleveland, USA
23 July, Mohengan Sun Arena, Uncasville, USA
25 July, TD Garden, Boston, USA
26 July, Prudential Center, Newark, USA
28 July, Barclays Center, New York City, USA
30 July, Wells Fargo Center, Philadelphia, USA
31 July, Verizon Center, Washington DC, USA
2 August, Bridgestone Arena, Nashville, USA
4 August, American Airlines Center, Dallas, USA
5 August, Toyota Center, Houston, USA

Europe

1 November, O2 Area, Prague, Czech Republic
2 November, Olympiahalle, Munich, Germany
4 November, Laszlo Papp Budapest Sports Arena, Budapest, Hungary
6 November, Atlas Arena, Lodz, Poland
8 November, Wiener Stadthalle, Vienna, Austria
10 November, Unipol Arena, Bologna, Italy
12 November, Galaxie Amneville, Amneville, France
13 November, Ziggo Dome, Amsterdam, Netherlands
17 November, Zalgiris Arena, Kaunas, Lithuania

19 November, Hartwell Arena, Helsinki, Finland
21 November, Friends Arena, Stockholm, Sweden
22 November, Royal Arena, Copenhagan, Denmark
25 November, 3Arena, Dublin, Ireland
26 November, SSE Arena, Belfast, Northern Ireland
28 November, Echo Arena, Liverpool, England
30 November, Arena Birmingham, Birmingham, England
1 December, Metro Radio Arena, Newcastle, England
3 December, SSE Hydro, Glasgow, Scotland

Rhapsody Tour Typical Set List

Now I'm Here
Seven Seas of Rhye
Keep Yourself Alive
Hammer to Fall
Killer Queen
Don't Stop Me Now
In the Lap of the Gods...Revisited
Somebody to Love
The Show Must Go On
I'm In Love With My Car
Bicycle Race
Another One Bites the Dust
Machines (Or 'Back to Humans')
I Want It All
Love of My Life
39
Doing All Right
Crazy Little Thing Called Love
Under Pressure
I Want to Break Free
You Take My Breath Away
Who Wants to Live Forever
Last Horizon (Brian May cover)
Tie Your Mother Down
Fat Bottomed Girls
Radio Ga Ga
Bohemian Rhapsody

Encores:
Ay-Oh
We Will Rock You
We Are the Champions
God Save The Queen

5 December, Motorpoint Arena, Nottingham, England
6 December, First Direct Arena, Leeds, England
8 December, Fly DSA Arena, Sheffield, England
9 December, Manchester Arena, Manchester, England
12-13 December, O2 Arena, London, England
15 December, Wembley Arena, London, England
16 December, Arena Birmingham, Birmingham, England

2018

Oceania
17-18 February, Spark Arena, Auckland, New Zealand
21-22 February, Qudos Bank Arena, Sydney, Australia
24 February, Brisbane Entertainment Centre, Brisbane,

Australia
27-28 February, Adelaide Entertainment Centre, Adelaide, Australia
2-3 March, Rod Laver Arena, Melbourne, Australia
6 March, Perth Arena, Perth, Australia

Europe
7 June, Altice Arena, Lisbon, Portugal
9 June, WiZink Center, Madrid, Spain
10 June, Palau Sant Jordi, Barcelona, Spain
13 June, Lanxess Arena, Cologne, Germany
15 June, Jyske Bank Boxen, Herning, Denmark
17 June, Telenor Arena, Olso, Norway,
19 June, Mercedes Benz Arena, Berlin, Germany
20 June, Barclaycard Arena, Hamburg, Germany
25 June, Mediolanum Forum, Milan, Italy
27 June, Rotterdam Ahoy, Rotterdam, Netherlands
29 June, Sportspaleis, Antwerp, Belgium
1 July, Wembley Arena, London, England
2 July, O2 Arena, London, England
4 July, O2 Arena, London, England
6 July, Glasgow Green, Glasgow, Scotland
8 July, Marlay Park, Dublin, Ireland

The Crown Jewels
1/2/5/7/8/14/15/19/21/22 September, The Park Theater, Las Vegas, USA

QUEEN
+ Adam Lambert

NORTH AMERICAN TOUR
2017

Rhapsody Tour 2019/20

2019

North America

10 July, Rogers Arena, Vancouver, Canada
12 July, Tacoma Dome, Tacoma, USA
14 July, SAP Center, San Jose, USA
16 July, Talking Stick Resort Arena, Phoenix, USA
17 July, Las Vegas Festival Grounds, Las Vegas, USA
19-20 July, The Forum, Inglewood, USA
23 July, American Airlines Center, Dallas, USA
24 July, Toyota Center, Houston, USA
27 July, Little Caesars Arena, Detroit, USA
28 July, Scotiabank Arena, Toronto, Canada
30 July, Capital One Arena, Washington DC, USA
31 July, PPG Paints Arena, Pittsburgh, USA
3 August, Wells Fargo Center, Philadelphia, USA
4 August, Xfinity Center, Mansfield, USA
6-7 August, Madison Square Garden, New York City, USA
9 August, United Center, Chicago, USA
10 August, Xcel Engergy Center, Saint Paul, USA
13 August, Nationwide Arena, Columbus, USA
15 August, Bridgestone Arena, Nashville, USA
17 August, BB&T Center, Sunrise, USA
18 August, Amalie Arena, Tampa, USA
20 August, Smoothie King Center, New Orelans, USA
22 August, State Farm Arena, Atlanta, USA
23 August, Spectrum Center, Charlotte, USA
28 September, Central Park, New York City, USA

2020

Asia

18-19 January, Gocheok Sky Dome, Seoul, South Korea
25-26 January, Saitama Super Arena, Saitama, Japan
28 January, Kyocera Dome, Osaka, Japan
30 January, Nagoya Dome, Nagoya, Japan

Oceania

5 February, Westpac Stadium, Wellington, New Zealand
7 February, Mount Smart Stadium, Auckland, New Zealand
10 February, Forsyth Barr Stadium, Dunedin, New Zealand
13 February, Suncorp Stadium, Brisbane, Australia
15-16 February, ANZ Stadium, Sydney, Australia
19-20 February, AAMI Park, Melbourne, Australia
23 February, Optus Stadium, Perth, Australia
26 February, Adelaide Oval, Adelaide, Australia
29 February, Metricon Stadium, Gold Coast, Australia

QUEEN LIVE
COLLECTED

R oger Taylor and Brian May can never have imagined they would find their next frontman at the 2009 final of US TV talent show, 'American Idol'. The duo made a guest appearance and were blown away by the talent of 26-year-old California boy Adam Lambert, who incidentally, had sung 'Bohemian Rhapsody' for his very first audition piece on the reality show. Lambert and fellow finalist Kris Allen sang 'We Are the Champions', accompanied by Taylor and May. It was the soulful Allen who became American Idol champion but uber-theatrical runner-up Lambert ultimately bagged the bigger prize. That of Queen vocalist.

'We didn't ask for him, we didn't look for him, he just turned up,' said Brian. 'And he could do everything. He's a born exhibitionist. He's not Freddie, and he's not pretending to be him but he has a parallel set of equipment.'

Brian and Roger didn't immediately approach Adam.

'Amongst of the furore of the final, there wasn't really a quiet moment to talk,' said Brian May. 'But Roger and I are definitely hoping to have a meaningful conversation with him at some point. It's not like we, as Queen, would rush into coalescing with another singer just like that. It isn't that easy.'

Adam had commitments as 'American Idol' runner-up but in November 2011 he joined Brian and Roger for a special performance at the MTV Europe Awards in Belfast. A month later, the three began formal discussions with a view to Adam fronting Queen in concert. There were some who voiced concerns at the choice, given Adam's start on reality TV. Brian, however, swiftly shot them down.

'I've not always been positive about shows like that but there is no doubt that it offers a door to some real genuine talent along the way. If you have enough talent and enough will to succeed, you will get there by whatever route presents itself. Once you have scaled the castle walls, with the sword in your hand, it matters little how you got there.'

The new front man, who in the previous few years had earned his rock star stripes by recording a solo album and touring, was charmingly humble to be joining the Queen 'family'.

'I wish that it was still Freddie up there,' he said, 'but since he's not with us I'm really happy to take the job.'

Adam Lambert and Brian May on stage at HMV
Hammersmith Apollo, July 11, 2012, London, UK

On 6 March 2014, Queen + Adam Lambert announced their intention to tour North America that June and July, starting in Chicago and including concerts at the legendary Madison Square Garden in New York and the Forum in Los Angeles where the band had last performed in 1982. A month later, it was announced that they would play in South Korea for the first time ever at the Super Sonic Festival and also play several dates in Japan. Dates in Australia and New Zealand were then made public. Finally, the European and South American legs were announced. The tour would prove to be a huge success – as described by a reviewer in 'Rolling Stone' magazine.

'From his cheeky call-and-response during "Another One Bites the Dust" to his outsize take on "Killer Queen," spreading out on a purple lounger and fake-chugging champagne, Lambert proved as brilliant a fill-in as you're bound to find. "Somebody to Love" was goose bump-inducing thanks to Lambert's vocal acrobatics. And that's to say nothing of his vocal magic during "Bohemian Rhapsody" and "We Are the Champions." Queen don't skimp on spectacle. They put on a rock show that often feels more like a Vegas spectacle. Dizzying, rainbow stage lights: check. Red-and-green laser lights draping the entire arena in a Christmas hue: surely. A floating drum riser from which Taylor smacked the skins during a thrashing encore rendition of "We Will Rock You"? Of course. A gold glitter shower to close out the evening? How could they

Adam Lambert performs with Queen at the SAP Center
on July 1, 2014 in San Jose, California

not? These flourishes were always for the best. Beyond the classics, Queen earned a huge response from tracks like the slinky soiree "Who Wants to Live Forever," the Broadway-esque "The Show Must Go On" and the swaying "In the Lap of the Gods." Their greatest undertaking? A reinterpretation of Mercury's "Love Kills," a 1984 solo track that the frontman made with Giorgio Moroder for a restored version of the 1927 silent film 'Metropolis'. Here, the band slowed it down, performing as a trio at the front of the catwalk. Lambert's vocals hung just below the upper-deck risers - "Bless him," he said in a toast to Mercury. "But we do a version of this our way". Lambert made the headlines, but his vocals would have nowhere to sit if Brian May and Roger Taylor weren't such pros. Last night, the former channelled David Gilmour during a brilliant extended guitar intro to "Tie Your Mother Down" and unleashed far more thrash and distortion then many would have expected. The latter, meanwhile, kept his sticks on the pulse all evening, dropping smacking martial beats during "Another One Bites the Dust" and "Radio Ga Ga." Let's be honest: What's a Queen show without some spectacular outfits? By our count, Lambert wore eight different ones during the two-hour gig. His bandmates? They stuck to more traditional attire — shirt and slacks — but don't worry: May did don a gold cape during "Bohemian Rhapsody." It was only fitting.

'As had always been customary, no Queen show was complete without an extravagant stage set. Their Summer Festival Tour of 2016 did not disappoint. The shows were suitably replete with lights, lasers, a giant mirror ball, fireworks and glitter - plus multiple costume changes for Adam and a flowing silver cloak for Brian. Of the 23 performances, the one closing the iconic Isle of Wight festival was arguably the most memorable. Queen had never played it before.

'When I think of The Isle of Wight Festival I think of Hendrix, Dylan and The Who,' said Roger Taylor shortly before the gig. 'What immortal company to be in! Queen are thrilled to be there and can promise a special night.'

It was that all right - as shown by the review in the UK's Daily Telegraph newspaper.

'The sheer quality and enduring appeal of the songs trounced all cynicism. And in Lambert they have a charismatic and unique frontman

who, to his credit, acknowledged early on that there is only one Freddie Mercury ("You're all thinking it," he said). They opened with "One Vision". Although grey of locks, May can still crunch those riffs out. Lambert, looking like Faith-era George Michael, preened and prowled. You'd suspect Mercury would approve of him: he was refreshingly arch and theatrical. After "Fat Bottomed Girls", he looked into the crowd and spat: "All those fat arsed bitches out there, get on your bikes and ride!". There wasn't really a song that couldn't be labelled classic. You were reminded of Queen's scope: the metal of "Stone Cold Crazy", the disco of "Another One Bites the Dust", and the pure pop of "I Want To Break Free". And then there were the anomalies... "Don't Stop Me Now" is a Queen song that was once derided but has grown in popularity over the years. Youngsters in the crowd lapped it up, shouting every word.

Roger Taylor — supplemented on drums by his son Rufus — sang vocals on "A Kind of Magic". He made a good fist of it but it was clear why he's a drummer. Mercury appeared on screen twice: once to duet with May on "Love of My Life" and again to sing the second verse of "Bohemian Rhapsody". Credit must be given to the band for not over-egging things. The balance was tasteful. After a finale of "We Will Rock You" and "We Are the Champions", gold confetti burst over the crowd to the National Anthem which closes every Queen show.'

The tour proved, without a shadow of a doubt, that Adam Lambert was now a fully paid-up member of the Queen family.

'I call him the Miracle Man,' said Brian May during a TV interview mid-tour. 'He was gifted to us. He is the reason that we are still alive as a functioning rock band.' In January 2017 Queen + Adam Lambert announced they were taking to the road again, beginning in North America in late June. Three months later, in April, they confirmed a series of European dates for November and December, followed by an announcement of performances in Australia and New Zealand in February and March 2018. A second European leg of the tour was added for later that year, in addition to a 10-night residency, entitled 'The Crown Jewels' at the Park Theater, Las Vegas, USA in September 2018.

Before the American dates, there was a change of personnel. Roger's

son, percussionist Rufus, confirmed that he would not be touring with the band, citing schedule conflicts with his band The Darkness. His place was taken by long-time Queen Extravaganza drummer Tyler Warren.

The tour itself promised a make-over, too.

'The tour will look entirely different to the show we took around before in 2014,' revealed Roger Taylor. 'Production has really changed a lot, the things you can do now, you have a much broader palette, the technology has really come along. But we don't use it all. We don't play to click track. It's 100% live. We're planning on doing stuff we either haven't done before or haven't done for a long time. We started as an albums band, that's what we were. The fact we had hits was just a bi-product.'

Adam Lambert also suggested surprises were in store.

'What people should know if they came to the shows a couple of years back, is obviously we will still be playing the big hit songs you know and love from Queen, but we thought it would be good to challenge ourselves a bit,' he explained. 'Change it up a little bit, change the visuals, change all the technology, change the set list to some degree. We will probably be pulling some other songs out of the Queen catalogue which we haven't done before, which I am very excited about.'

These other Queen songs would include 'Hammer to Fall', 'Get Down, Make Love', 'The Bicycle Song' and 'I'm In Love with My Car'. One of Adam's own songs, 'Two Fux', was added to the set list for the first time.

The production values and stage set could hardly have been more spectacular, with homage paid to the 40th anniversary release of Queen's sixth album 'News of the World. The head of 'Frank' - the robot gracing the album's cover – was recreated in giant 3-D form, looming above the band as they performed 'Killer Queen', one of the songs 'pulled out of the Queen catalogue'. The main stage, measuring 21m wide by 34m long and boasting, was in the shape of a guitar body – an

ode to Brian's iconic custom-made 'Red Special'. Extending from this was a 20m runway, mimicking the neck of the instrument. This led to the B-stage which was in the shape of the guitar head and fitted with a prop lift which was used during 'Bicycle Race' where Lambert rode his bike around to the beat of the song. Over 60lbs of glitter was added the custom-made paint covering the stage in order to provide extra sparkle. Highlights of spectacular included Brian May being elevated above the stage as he performed a mind-bending guitar solo in space and a Metropolis-esque backdrop packed full of flashing lights and exploding smoke cannons for smash hit 'Radio Ga Ga'.

The words of one reviewer said it all. . .

'With fantastic players, a dazzling stage design, an almost unparalleled catalogue of classic songs, and an outstanding frontman, Queen still offer one of the most entertaining nights of rock and roll to be seen and heard anywhere.'

Hot on the heels of the success of the film 'Bohemian Rhapsody', Queen + Adam Lambert announced that they would tour North America in the summer of 2019, followed by a second Asian leg, a third taking in Australia and New Zealand, and, in the Spring of 2020, a fourth leg around Europe. The 'Rhapsody' tour was a brand-new production, which according to the press release, would be 'as experimental and rule-defying as the hit-packed Queen back catalogue.'

'This is a great opportunity,' said Brian May. 'Our last tour featured our most ambitious production ever, and got us our best notices ever. So, we decided to rip it apart and get even more ambitious! Watch out, America!'

The set truly was ambitious, comprising of three separate 'worlds' based on the aesthetic of three of Queen's classic albums – 'Night at the Opera', 'The Works' and 'The Game'. The show opened in the grand surroundings of a golden, baroque-style opera house, moving on to a grittier, retro, futuristic industrial space before ending in a more conventional concert environment. The stage featured two lifts used within the show to bring members of the band from under the stage or to elevate them above it. A 45 metre catwalk extended from the mainstage to a B-stage.

Adam Lambert during the performance at Palau Sant Jordi in Barcelona, Spain, on May 22, 2016

Before the group even began the show, an image of a crown donned the stage as smoke danced around it. A closer look revealed intricate pieces of the band's history, including May's 'Red Special' guitar and an iconic shot of Mercury performing. Once Queen and Lambert began, the crown became even more mesmerizing, slowly lifting to the summit of the stage. Other highlights included Adam Lambert posing on a blinged-up motor bike as he sang 'The Bicycle Song' and, in a nod to Brian May's astrophysicist pedigree, his lengthy guitar solo played atop screens projecting meteoric and interstellar imagery. Meanwhile planet-like orbs floated overhead. Then there was May's 'Bohemian Rhapsody' solo which he performed in an iridescent bionic suit and mask.

A US review proclaimed: 'It's hard to imagine a more tasteful way for a band with nothing to prove to carry on decades after losing one of the most singular frontmen in rock history. But the Queen + Adam Lambert experience fits like a pair of the authoritative singer's gold-laced gloves. Don't stop 'em now.'

However, at the end of February 2020 they had no choice but to stop. After completing the Oceanic leg of the tour, they flew home and, due to the COVID 19 pandemic, had no choice but to cancel their forthcoming European gigs.

'After starting off 2020 with an amazing run of shows playing to audiences of upwards of 50,000 in a single night, the cancellation of the Europe shows that should have followed last summer was a huge disappointment,' said Brian May in early 2021. 'Those incredible scenes at those concerts now seem like an impossibly distant dream. One minute we are out in Australia strutting our stuff and interacting with thousands of happy people, next minute we are stuck in the house. We were so lucky to be able to complete that leg of the tour, running just ahead of the wave that was about to break on us.'

With the pandemic still raging, the band decided to postpone their outstanding 'Rhapsody' performances until 2022.

'We wish to make it clear,' came the announcement, 'none of the shows from 2020 and 2021 have been cancelled, just re-arranged due to COVID-19. We really do hope that as many people as possible who were booked for those original dates in 2020 will still be able to join us for the shows.'

Staying engaged with their fans, the band then returned to YouTube with a Tour Watch Party offering highlights of Queen + Adam Lambert performances from previous tours and festival gigs. The enthusiastic response led directly to the compilation, mixing, and release of their first album together, 'Live Around the World', presented in CD, DVD, Blu-ray and vinyl packages. A concert version of the movie also became available to stream via download.

'As we all grapple with the challenge of creating live shows in a world dominated by a formidable viral enemy, it seemed the perfect time for us to create a collection of hand-picked live highlights from our Queen shows over the last seven years with our brother Adam Lambert,' said the band when the 'Live Around the World' was released in late 2020. 'As you watch and listen to these tracks, you'll be journeying all around the world with us and experiencing a complete virtual live set.'

In addition to pleasing the fans. 'Live Around the World' gave Queen + Adam Lambert a No 1 album on week of release in the UK and elsewhere around the world – marking Queen's first UK No 1 album in 25 years, their 10th in total, and Adam's first time at the top of the chart. But they cannot wait to get back on stage.

'When we do eventually get to play in front of live audiences it will be with a ferociously renewed attack,' says Roger Taylor. 'And we shall revel in the wonderful experience of actually interacting with them again.'

The postponement of the tour dates in 2021 was especially disappointing for the band as the year marks Queen's Golden Jubilee – 1971 being the year that John Deacon was recruited, completing the band's classic line-up. Nevertheless, The Show Must Go On – and it will in 2022 when Queen + Adam Lambert return to touring and embark on their next chapter together. . .

Adam Lambert and Brian May on stage at Mediolanum Forum on June 25, 2018 in Milan, Italy

Post Script

Freddie Mercury passed away on 24th November 1991 from an AIDS related illness. He was 45. On the night he died, his broken-hearted band mates - Brian May, Roger Taylor and John Deacon - first conceived the idea of a memorial concert to be held in his honour. This finally came to pass when The Freddie Mercury Tribute: A Concert for AIDs awareness was staged at Wembley Stadium on April 20 1992. Artists taking part with the three remaining members of Queen included Def Leppard, Roger Daltry, Robert Plant, Ian Hunter, Axl Rose, Elton John and George Michael. It was Michael's rendition of 'Somebody to Love' that stole the show - just as Queen had stolen Live Aid. 'It was,' said the late, former Wham singer, 'the proudest moment of my career.'

In May 2002, 'We Will Rock You', a musical theatre production based on the music of Queen, opened at London's Dominium theatre. It ran for 12 years and continues to tour around the world.

'Free' and 'Bad Company' vocalist Paul Rodgers toured with Brian May and Roger Taylor as 'Queen with Paul Rodgers' from 2004-2009. John Deacon retired in 1997 and so didn't take part.

'American Idol' runner-up Adam Lambert began singing with May and Taylor in 2011. Known as 'Queen with Adam Lambert', they continue to tour the world.

'Bohemian Rhapsody', a 2018 biographical film about Freddie Mercury and Queen, saw actor Remi Malek, who played Freddie Mercury, winning a Golden Globe and an Academy Award for his performance. The movie broke box office records across the world on its release.